PEST CONTROL

C.D. Habecker and Luna Nyx

A NineStar Press Publication
www.ninestarpress.com

Pest Control

© 2021 C.D. Habecker and Luna Nyx
Cover Art © 2021 Natasha Snow
Edited by Elizabetta McKay

This is a work of fiction. Names, characters, places, and incidents are either the product of the author's imagination or are used fictitiously. Any resemblance to actual persons living or dead, business establishments, events, or locales is entirely coincidental.

All rights reserved. No part of this publication may be reproduced in any material form, whether by printing, photocopying, scanning or otherwise without the written permission of the publisher. To request permission and all other inquiries, contact NineStar Press at the physical or web addresses above or at Contact@ninestarpress.com.

ISBN: 978-1-64890-398-4

First Edition, October, 2021

Also available in eBook, ISBN: 978-1-64890-397-7

CONTENT WARNING:

This book contains sexually explicit content, which is only suitable for mature readers. Depictions of panic attacks and social anxiety, depression, starvation, illness, ableism, past trauma; animals hunted for food; discussion of homophobia.

Rhys has a simple life in the backwoods. All he needs is his trusty compound bow, impressive book collection, warm cabin, full food cellar, and himself. So, when Rhys discovers a sly wolf stealing his kills, which are supposed to last him through the coming winter, he's forced to set a trap and kill the pest.

But, instead of the wolf, Rhys finds a mysterious (and naked) man named Everett.

After learning Everett has nowhere else to go, Rhys hesitantly invites him to stay and heal. But he doesn't get much time to adjust to life with his eccentric (and stupidly handsome) house guest, not when winter arrives early and with a vengeance.

Cooped up in the cabin together for months, will Rhys learn to love himself and another? Or will hidden truths and empty stomachs snuff out the flames of love and life?

For all the queer people out there. I hope you know that you're loved and worth it.

Chapter One

Rhys pulled the string of his compound bow back taut, his hands steady as he readied his arrow. Tucked as he was behind the thick foliage, the buck's tawny coat was well camouflaged in the autumn hues, making aiming for his target difficult. Though, it also benefited Rhys; combined with being downwind of the magnificent creature, the foliage kept him just as hidden.

The buck, completely unaware of his presence, stepped out enough to bend its graceful neck to drink from the trickling stream. Still on guard, cautious as animals of prey always were, its ears flickered at the tiniest of noises, its muscles tensed and ready for flight at any moment.

Rhys had only one chance at getting this right.

One wrong move, and the buck—a good month's worth of venison dinners—would disappear into the forest, never to be seen again.

This wasn't Rhys's first rodeo, not in the slightest, yet he couldn't help the nervous hitch in his quiet, slow breathing when it seemed, for a moment, that the buck had seen him. Its head jerked up and turned, dark eyes looking straight in his direction. It didn't flee, only stared ominously as if caught in a truck's headlights. Rhys knew he wouldn't get a better chance than this one.

It was always a strange feeling to look into the eyes of his prey, of something he was going to kill. Ignoring the shudder that rolled down his spine, he took the shot anyway. Releasing his grip on the string, he allowed his arrow to take flight in a silent, quick *whirr* through the air.

Before the buck could even blink in reaction, the sharp metal arrowhead lodged deep where the shoulder of its front leg met its torso, cutting through thick layers of fur, skin, fat, and muscle—and hopefully its heart or lung, maybe even shattering its shoulder. Rhys had counted on his aim making the cleanest, quickest kill, one that would keep the animal's suffering at a minimum.

The buck immediately took off running down the stream with a loud startled noise, and so did Rhys, chasing after his wounded prey. Still much faster than he was, even with its injury, the buck disappeared into the trees. Leaving a trail of blood and crushed foliage in its hasty retreat, it led the hunter on through the forest for what seemed like at least a good few miles.

But, when Rhys finally made it to the end of the blood trail, there was no buck in sight, only pools of blood mixed in with the muddy ground, and hoofprints leading off deeper into the forest, away from the stream. Rhys furrowed his eyebrows as he knelt beside them and traced their outline with his fingers.

Not hoofprints, he realized with an angry huff—*wolf prints*, and familiar ones at that, the large canine's paws unmistakable to his trained eyes. Streaks of blood followed alongside them, which left Rhys with only one answer.

"It's *you* again, huh?" he grumbled through gritted teeth, digging his fingers into the wet mud, replacing the print with his own.

This wasn't the first time the wolf had stolen his kill. In fact, it was the fifth time this season. Rhys thought that by traveling far in the opposite direction he normally took toward his trusty hunting perch, he'd be able to avoid the bane of his existence, but yet again, he had been outsmarted.

It was as if the thieving canine had been following him, *stalking* him even, to drag away his kills, mooching off of his hard work and dedication. The reoccurring situation pissed him off to no end, especially when winter was only a mere month or two away from turning the landscape white and cold.

He needed this kill, needed the other four lost kills as well, to keep himself from starving in the dead of winter when it would be next to impossible to do any sort of hunting. This late in the game, his food storage cellar should be full already; he shouldn't have spent all of his time hunting when firewood and water needed to be collected and stored, and his fall vegetable harvest needed to be pickled.

With how things were looking now, it was loud and clear: Rhys was utterly and completely *fucked*.

★

It took Rhys two whole days of hammering down scrap metal over the hot flames in his fireplace, but finally, the project was completed. Now, Rhys was back to march on into the forest, this time with ten heavy wolf traps in his backpack, clanging together noisily.

He hated that it had come to this, but the wolf had left him with no other options. If it wasn't going to peacefully cooperate with him and share the forest's resources like every other predator, then Rhys would have to take it out. And, he wouldn't mind a fluffy wolf pelt to keep him nice and toasty.

Rhys set the traps up around his usual hunting locations, baiting each one with a scrap of rabbit meat—the only game he'd successfully hunted this season, along with fish and other small creatures he'd easily caught in simple snares. It was a bit of a long shot that this wolf would be dumb enough to step right into the trap, but Rhys thought it might work, given how gluttonous the predator seemed to be.

Or, at least, he hoped and prayed with all he had that it would work.

Rhys's anxiousness kept him up later than usual that night with his windows wide open, unable to sleep at all, listening for the telltale howl or yelp of a caught, injured wolf in the distance. As much as Rhys absolutely *hated* the creature, he wanted to make sure he could immediately put it out of its misery instead of letting it wallow in excruciating pain for hours.

The sun had just begun to rise from its slumber when he finally heard it—the long-awaited howl breaking through the tense silence. Despite his grogginess from lack of sleep, all tiredness was lost at the sound, replaced with a straight shot of adrenaline pumping through Rhys's veins. He jolted up in his bed, heart racing a mile a minute, hastily pulled on his boots, and took off into the forest toward the source of the noise. The eerie silence had returned, only broken by the sound of twigs snapping under his boots. Rhys worried that, somehow, the wolf might have broken free from the sharp teeth of the trap.

"Please still be there, please still be there, *please*," he prayed under panted-out breaths, almost tripping over a fallen tree in his hurry.

With white knuckles, Rhys gripped his shotgun, a weapon he only used in case of extreme emergencies, since it was much harder to craft replacement bullets than the arrows for his bow. He was fully prepared to riddle the unlucky predator's body full of lead and holes. But what he found was most definitely not what he expected: it was *not* a wolf.

"Wait, wait, *fuck*, don't shoot!" the man pleaded, hands raised in the air in frantic surrender. "Don't shoot! Please, don't kill me!"

Rhys dropped his gun, letting it fall to the ground with a dull clatter. He couldn't believe his eyes—was he dreaming? Had he ended up falling asleep after all, and was now experiencing a sick nightmare? Why was a human, with his bloody, mangled leg, caught in the wolf trap? And why the hell was he butt-fucking *naked*?

"Uh," Rhys gulped, averting his eyes from the man's junk, his gaze flickering down to give a concerned look to where the trap met skin. It looked absolutely *nasty*, steel teeth dug deep into the flesh, almost all the way through to hints of pale, white bone. And sure, he'd seen his fair share of gross carcasses before, whether during butchering or coming across a bear's leftovers, yet his stomach rumbled with a wave of nausea. "A-are you okay?"

"Of course I'm not fucking *okay*!" the man squawked, bringing Rhys's attention up to his face—a surprisingly handsome face, despite the dusting of dried mud on his dark skin and twigs stuck in his messy, bird's-nest head of coiled black hair. "Why are you just standing there! Help me, please!"

"R-right, shit, s-sorry."

Rhys cringed inwardly at his awkward stuttering. He knelt to stick a key into the trap, and the jaws snapped open with a sickening squelch.

The man let out a hiss of pain as he pulled his injured leg toward him. "*Fuck*, this is really bad. How am I going to be able to walk now?"

"I'm sorry," Rhys said again like a broken record. "Y-you're definitely going to need stitches for that. Do...do you need me to call a hospital? I got a phone back at my cabin—there's no cell service up here, but if I drive down the mountain, there will be. I'm sure they can send over a helicopter and take you back—"

"No!" the man interrupted with a harsh shake of his head. "No. No hospitals!"

He attempted to stand up, scrambling like a newborn deer, only to let out a pained yelp when his injured leg couldn't bear his weight. It buckled beneath him, wobbling precariously. But before he could hit the ground, Rhys quickly reached an arm out to stabilize him.

"Okay, okay, no hospitals, I promise. Just calm down, all right? You're going to hurt yourself even more doing shit like that."

Rhys grunted with effort as he hoisted the man's body up to fully support him like a human crutch.

"Just leave me here to die," the man groaned, letting his head loll back to rest on Rhys's shoulder.

A moment of panic rushed through Rhys when the man's eyelids grew heavy, and he worried if he didn't get help soon, he would surely pass out or even die from the blood loss.

"No can do, stranger," Rhys sighed, slapping the man's face softly to hopefully get some color and consciousness back. He only received a flutter of eyelids in response, the man's dark irises looking up at him in a daze, and it was nothing short of *extremely* concerning. "Come on; how about we go back to my cabin? I'm no doctor, but I've dealt with my own injuries before. You'll probably be just fine with some stitches and rest, okay? How does that sound?"

Rhys once again received no answer aside from an incoherent throaty grumble, so he took that as the best confirmation he'd get out of the poor man. Thankfully, he wasn't much heavier than the logs Rhys had once dragged out from the forest to build his cabin.

Rhys was thankful to finally reach his cabin and soon had the stranger laid out on his bed next to a roaring fire, a blanket draped over him, hoping to warm the eerily lifeless body that felt much too cold to the touch. He'd lost so much blood Rhys was far from convinced he'd live to see another day. But since his heart still beat weakly in his chest, there was a glimmer of hope for his survival—as long as Rhys wasn't about to mess it up, of course.

The festering leg wound had finally stopped oozing, leaving a crusty mess of dried blood and caked-on mud that had Rhys's empty stomach acid gurgling in protest.

He was glad he hadn't had a chance to eat breakfast because he'd surely have puked it out by now. Rhys put his own feelings aside as best as he could and focused on taking deep, calming breaths as he gently cleaned the injury with a rag soaked in a saltwater concoction he hoped would be enough to wash out the bacteria.

When he had finished, Rhys moved on to the most crucial step: stitching up the wound. He'd done it a few times to himself, but only for shallow, superficial cuts. By the time the task was completed, he'd spent an entire hour stitching up the gaping, deep wound. The result wasn't pretty in the slightest, though it would have to do. He'd carefully dressed the man in his own clothes, which covered it up, anyway. Thankfully, since Rhys preferred his clothing to fit oversized, they fit nicely on the man, despite him being a larger size.

The morning was still young, with the sun not even finished rising over the horizon, but the combination of lack of sleep and taking care of the injured stranger had exhausted Rhys. He swore he'd only close his eyes for a moment, just a second—but as soon as his head hit the cozy pile of furs on the floor, he was out like a light, dreaming of wolves and a nameless man with dark eyes.

Chapter Two

Three days. Three whole days it took for the stranger to wake up. Three days that Rhys spent pacing back and forth in the small confines of his cabin, anxious out of his mind that the steady rise and fall of the man's chest would stop, leaving him to deal with a dead body and an immense amount of guilt. Three days Rhys could have spent making up for his food deficit, instead of wasting what remained of autumn on monitoring him. Three days he wrestled with his conscience, debating whether he should ignore the stranger's plea to stay away from hos-pitals. If he'd been stuck in a comatose state for any longer, Rhys would have had no choice but to act against his wishes and drive him down to civilization. Thankfully, though, it wasn't necessary.

The stranger let out a soft groan, making his awakening known, and Rhys paused his pacing and whirled around to see the man slowly sitting up.

"Wh-where am I?" he asked hoarsely. He looked around for a few moments before letting out a screech when his wide eyes landed on Rhys. "Oh! It's y-*you*! The hunter! Sh-shit, why—*what*—"

He quickly shuffled backward to shove himself into the corner. His breath quickened audibly, and his gaze darted around as if he were searching for an escape route.

"Relax, relax, it's okay! You're going to reopen your wound if you move around too much." Rhys raised his hands in the air and took a few cautious steps back as if facing a flighty, terrified animal. "I know you don't want to go to hospitals, so don't worry; you're just in my cabin. Been here for the last three days healing after I stitched you all up. Don't you remember me saving you from that trap your leg got caught in?"

Gazing down at his injured leg, wrapped carefully with fabric, the man was silent for a few minutes. He took a series of deep breaths before returning his attention to Rhys.

"Yeah, shit, I remember. Sorry, I just…waking up here…thought you had taken me to a hospital."

Rhys lowered his hands slowly and stepped closer. "I get it—I would be terrified, too, waking up in a strange place. But don't worry. You're safe."

"Right, right, I'm safe…" the man whispered.

Again, the man was silent for a few minutes.

"Well, um, my name's Rhys Ortiz. What's yours, strange naked man I found in the forest?"

The corners of the man's lips twitched into a weak, pensive smile. "Everett. My name's Everett."

"Just Everett, huh? No last name?"

Everett blinked. "Uh…no?"

"Okay…well, nice to meet you, then, just Everett. How old are you? I'm twenty-five; you look like you're around my age." Rhys held out his hand for Everett to shake, but he only stared at it with narrowed eyes, so Rhys dropped it to his side awkwardly.

"I'm...uh...twenty."

"Ah, okay, I was a bit off then."

Silence, once more, until Everett's stomach growled quite loudly.

"Hungry, aren't you?" Rhys laughed at Everett's grimace.

He walked over to the pot hanging over the fire where he was heating up some rabbit stew for his own lunch. He plopped a heavy spoonful in a bowl and handed it to Everett, whose eyes lit up immediately at the savory, delicious scent. Without waiting for Rhys to give him a utensil to eat it with, Everett immediately tipped his head back and poured the steaming meal into his mouth, gulping it all down within mere seconds like a man starved. He even stuck his tongue out to lick the bowl clean, smearing broth on his rosy cheeks. When he deemed the bowl empty, he held it out to Rhys, who again filled it full of stew with a chuckle under his breath.

He ended up feeding Everett a total of six bowls, which drained the pot to only allow Rhys a single serving for himself. To be honest, he still felt a bit hungry. But Everett hadn't eaten for three whole days, so he needed the nutrients much more than Rhys.

"Well," Everett said, wringing his hands in his lap, "Thank you for everything. I really appreciate the food, the medical care, the clothes...but, I think it's time for me to go. I'd feel bad mooching off any more of your generosity."

Rhys waved his hand dismissively. "It's really no big deal. Do you have anywhere to go though? If it's far, I can drive you. I have my old truck parked in the shed out back; I haven't taken it out in a while, but it wouldn't be a big deal."

Everett dropped his gaze sheepishly to the floor and kicked at one of the loose wooden boards—enough of an answer for Rhys.

"I thought as much." Rhys sighed. "It's not really any of my business, but... Everett, are you running away from something? Or maybe...did you get kicked out?"

"Kind of" was all he mumbled.

Rhys didn't want to assume, but it made sense with Everett's condition, lack of clothes, and being so far out in the forest by himself, that something pretty bad had happened to him. He could only hope it wasn't super serious—that would've absolutely required getting the police involved, say if Everett had escaped some sort of fucked-up human trafficking operation. Or maybe, he was a murderer who'd shed his bloodstained clothes on the run from the murder scene—no, that couldn't be it. He seemed much too mild-mannered.

Being kicked out by his family didn't exactly explain Everett running around the woods naked, but Rhys hoped that was the case instead. It would've still sucked to be kicked out, though. Rhys was well aware of how it felt, having been thrust out of his childhood home a few years back.

And while he did want to know Everett's backstory, Rhys was careful not to pry any further, knowing all too well how embarrassing and downright depressing it could be to reveal such a thing, especially to a stranger like him.

It wasn't his place to know—all he needed to care about was how this poor guy had literally nowhere else to go. There was no way Rhys could even *consider* sending him back out into the forest or driving him down to the city. It would've been abandoning Everett to fend for himself, which he'd certainly fail at, thanks to the severity of his wound.

And so, there was only one clear solution.

"Everett, if you really have nowhere to go, you can always stay here."

His head snapped up, eyes wide in disbelief. "R-really?" he squeaked. "You'd let me stay here? I-I don't know if I can accept that. It's...too much!"

Though Rhys was a bit nervous about inviting a stranger into his home, he was willing to take the risk as he would've been ever so grateful if someone were to have done the same for him all those years ago.

Rhys shrugged. "It's no big deal. I've got enough room here for another person. And besides, you're still injured. It'll be at least a month until your leg heals. I'd rather you stay here—as long as you're okay with following my rules, and eating rabbits and fish rather than bigger game... I've been kind of unlucky this season," he added with a sigh, shaking his head as he remembered the true prey for his trap. "Some bastard wolf's been stealing all of my kills, so I don't have much red meat stocked up."

"O-oh, hah, that's too bad." Everett laughed nervously. Rhys thought he must not like wolves very much either. "W-well...if you're seriously offering this... I'd accept as long as I can give back to you somehow. I-is there anything I could do for you? Cook? Clean?"

Rhys hummed thoughtfully, drumming his fingers on the table. "Can you hunt at all?"

"Um...I've never hunted before." Everett frowned. "Is there anything else?"

"Well, that's no good. Everyone needs to know how to hunt!" Rhys declared with a firm nod. "I'll teach you, then, and once you're ready, you can help me stock up for winter."

Everett leaned forward, his eyes wide. "Really? You'll teach me how?"

"Yeah, yeah, I will. It's no problem. I could use a hand."

"Ooh, I'm so excited! Can we start hunting now?"

Before Everett could attempt to stand up on his one uninjured leg, Rhys grabbed him by the forearm with a chuckle.

"Whoa, where do you think you're going?" he asked with a raised brow. "I didn't mean we would start the lessons *now*. Did you forget you're still very injured?"

Everett made a low, frustrated grunting noise that sounded almost like a growl and glared down at his leg. "Okay, maybe not now, but how long do you think it'll take until we can start? Would I be better by tomorrow?"

Rhys couldn't help but snort. "No, not tomorrow. More like a few weeks. Everett, that trap dug so deep into your leg it hit the bone. It'll take much longer than a day to heal. Just be patient, okay? You can still help me with other tasks while we wait, though you should focus on resting so you can heal faster."

"Like what tasks?"

"Helping in the garden, maybe? I need to finish up the fall harvest soon and begin pickling the vegetables. There's also fishing, setting up rabbit snares, gathering firewood and water."

"Helping in the—that all sounds so *boring*," Everett whined.

Rhys let out a *tsk*, wagging his finger. "Don't be a brat already. I thought you said you wanted to help me?"

"I mean, I do want to help…"

Rhys leaned forward and ruffled his hair. "That's more like it. Now come on, how about you get some more rest?"

Chapter Three

Eight days later and closer to the inevitable winter, Everett had turned the hunter's quiet, lonely little life in the woods completely upside down and inside out.

At first, Rhys was appreciative of Everett assisting him with his chores, but he quickly learned it wasn't as much "help" as it was a hinderance, thanks to his injured leg. Instead of cleaning the dirt off the potatoes and carrots Rhys had been digging up from the garden, Everett ended up collapsing onto a pile of freshly picked apples, squishing half of them. Instead of sorting vegetables and meat into containers, somehow, Everett stumbled again and spilled brining liquid all over the floor. Instead of casting his fishing line into the river, he fell yet again and scared all of the fish away. And even when he was left in the cabin while Rhys went out to check his rabbit snares, chop firewood, and collect water, Everett managed to be an annoyance by attempting to heat up some lunch, but spilling half of the stew into the fireplace.

From thereon, he was banned from doing anything other than relaxing, which required Rhys to do a lot of reprimanding when Everett would frequently disobey, running outside—and falling—the second Rhys was out of sight.

In fact, Everett disobeyed practically every order and instruction Rhys gave, such as sleeping on the bed while Rhys took the floor.

During the late autumn and winter months, even with the mounds of blankets piled on top of him and the roaring fireplace, Rhys had always woken up cold and shivering. It wasn't pleasant, but he'd gotten used to it. So, when he awoke one morning the warmest he'd felt in months, his sleep-clouded mind thought it was somehow summer again—until he registered the hot puffs of breath hitting the back of his neck and an equally warm body curled around him. A heavy arm thrown over his waist trapped him there.

Immediately, the haze of sleep was blown away from Rhys's mind. It was as if he'd had a couple of shots of pure espresso, adrenaline thrumming through his veins as his body tensed, unsure whether to fight or take flight. He flickered his gaze around the log walls and the floor he had fallen asleep on. *Alone.* He'd insisted Everett sleep on the bed since he was the injured one. But instead, here he was, spooning Rhys like a lover might.

The position left Rhys with absolutely zero personal space, with his entire back plastered against his captor's chest, and claustrophobic, combined with the walls sandwiching him. The warmth that had been comforting during sleep quickly became too much, causing beads of sweat to gather on his forehead. Everett's body, his whistling breath, the slight scent of pine emanating from the soap used to wash their hair—holy shit, it was *way* too overwhelming for Rhys to handle after not having been touched by another human being in years.

"H-hey, creep, get off me!" Rhys shrieked, violently squirming like a fish out of water to turn to face Everett. With all the strength he could muster, he shoved the body off of him, sending Everett tumbling with a startled squeak, and then a pained groan when he smacked against the bed frame.

"What the hell—why'd you push me?" Everett rubbed at the back of his head as he sat up. He looked over with a tired frown, which Rhys met with a glare.

"Why the *fuck* were you cuddling with me?" Rhys shot back as he attempted to get his breathing under control. His hands shook as they gripped the fur blanket beneath him.

Everett shrugged sheepishly. "Because...you just looked so uncomfortable down there! You were shivering, and I felt bad! So, I moved down to cuddle you, and you seemed a lot more comfortable when I did. I thought I was doing a nice thing... What's so wrong with that?"

"What's so—Everett, it's weird to cuddle with *strangers*! We barely know each other! Why would I be comfortable with a stranger cuddling me? Without even asking? Have you ever fucking heard of personal space?"

"I-I... It was a normal thing for my family, especially when it was cold," Everett said in a small voice, with wide eyes, as if the idea of not doing so was foreign to him.

He looked so incredibly confused, and even a little bit frightened, which made Rhys feel bad for chewing him out so much. In his own family, they barely hugged each other, but he could understand where Everett was coming from. In fact, he was a bit jealous. Maybe if his parents had hugged him, he wouldn't be such a mess of a person.

Rhys sighed. "Well, we aren't family, Everett. And, you should really be caring more about your own well-being, especially over mine. You shouldn't be sleeping on the floor, okay? If you want to heal fast, then you need to sleep on the bed like I told you to."

"But why do *you* have to sleep on the floor? It's not good for you either! You can't expect me to be okay with not only taking your bed, but also making you freeze. Can't you just...sleep on the bed with me? I promise I won't cuddle you." He patted the bed. "It's big enough for the both of us."

Rhys eyed the bed suspiciously. It was no tiny twin-sized mattress, but it was barely big enough to be considered a queen. If he were to lie down next to Everett's larger body, they'd at least be touching arms. He attempted to imagine what it would be like. Would he even be able to fall asleep with a person beside him, probably shifting around and making noise? He'd never slept next to his past boyfriends as they'd always go home after their nightly escapades, so he wasn't sure. What if he were to awaken in Everett's arms again and be thrown into a panic attack?

On the other hand, the floor was also quite difficult to sleep on. During previous nights, Rhys had spent hours lying awake staring at the ceiling before he was able to drift off, thanks to the hard, cold wooden floors. His mattress was far more comfortable, possibly even enough to outweigh any potential disruptions from his guest. Combined with making sure Everett was comfortable and healing, sleeping in the bed might've been the better option.

"Fine, fine! I'll sleep with you on the damn bed as long as you keep that promise not to cuddle me," Rhys grumbled. "You promise you won't...right?"

Everett's face lit up as if he'd won a million dollars, and he nodded enthusiastically. "I promise!"

But of course, he didn't keep his promise. Every single morning after, Rhys would awaken in the same position. Yet as the days flew by, he found he was growing to enjoy waking up this way—though he'd never admit it aloud, especially to Everett. Now, eight days later, Rhys's body practically hummed with pleasure at being touched after going so long without, and he couldn't stop himself from nuzzling further into the comforting, warm embrace. He allowed himself a few more minutes of reveling in it before he forced himself to move.

"Everett, wake up," Rhys grumbled, "Come on—get your lazy ass up!"

Little goose bumps rose on Rhys's skin when Everett's long lashes fluttered open to tickle his neck.

"Go back to sleep. It's still early," Everett rasped sleepily as he tightened his grip, almost suffocating Rhys.

Rhys found it impossible to see out the window in this position, but the telltale light streaming in was enough to dispute Everett's claims. It must have been close to noon, not early in the slightest. Far too late, actually. Rhys was no morning person, but when there was so much to do and so few hours to do it all in, waking up this late was foolish. Even though their position was quite comfortable, Rhys couldn't spend all day like this.

"Nope, no more sleeping. We have shit to get done, don't you remember? I was going to start training you how to hunt today. Or...do you not want to anymore? I thought you were excited. But, okay, we don't—"

"Wait! I'm up, I'm up!" Everett shouted. "I still want to go, I swear!"

"Uh-huh, that's more like it," Rhys said with a sly grin. Stiff from sleep, he stood up and stretched his aching joints and muscles for a few minutes, before helping Everett up. "All right, let's start getting ready, then. We lost a lot of time by sleeping in so late. Are you going to need help getting dressed again?"

"No, I'm okay, but thanks," Everett said. "I've had, like...a week or something to recover. I should be better enough by now to at least put my own damn pants on."

Rhys chuckled at his huffy attitude. Everett was clearly frustrated at his temporary handicap, especially when he had to hold on to the table to keep his balance as he shimmied into his borrowed camouflage pants.

With all of the last week's failed chores in mind, Rhys wasn't sure about starting Everett's hunting training without evidence he was healed enough. But it was clear he couldn't keep Everett's energy contained much longer, especially now that he was building more strength. Rhys hoped today's plans would be enough; they certainly wouldn't be *exactly* what Everett was expecting.

It didn't take too much longer for the two to finish their morning routine. Thankfully, the sun was still high above them, leaving them with a good few hours of daylight. Despite Everett having to use one of Rhys's hiking sticks as a crutch, he practically bounced with pent-up energy and enthusiasm as they stepped out of the cabin into the afternoon sunlight.

"Excited, aren't you?" Rhys commented with a small, knowing smile.

"Of course I am! I've been stuck in that cabin for days, Rhys. *Days*!" Everett threw back his head dramatically. "And, honestly—not to shit on your cooking skills or anything, I swear—I'm getting pretty tired of fish and rabbits. I'd *die* for some deer right about now."

"You and me both. Just wait until winter comes—it's miserable being stuck in there for months. But, anyway... don't count on having any deer for tonight."

Everett stopped walking, a low whine filling the quiet forest that reminded Rhys vaguely of his childhood dog. "But, why? What do you mean, 'don't count on any deer for tonight'? I thought we were going hunting!"

"Yeah, uh, about that..." Rhys rubbed the back of his neck nervously. Everett's reaction was no surprise to him, but he didn't enjoy the pitiful look he received. "We aren't exactly going hunting today. It's going to be more like a training day. You need to learn how to hunt before you can actually hunt. There's a lot you need to learn, and there's no way I'm having you scare away all of our potential prey before you even know how to pull your own bowstring properly. And, not to mention, you're still gravely injured, Everett. You can't hunt like this. You can't even do anything without falling!"

"But...*Rhys*—"

"Nuh-uh, no 'buts,'" Rhys interrupted sternly, leaving no room for argument. "I'm the experienced hunter here, remember? So you, little *rookie*, need to follow my rules and instructions. It won't take long, if you're a good student, that is. We'll be eating deer in no time."

Everett looked ready to complain and stomp his one functional foot, but with a sharp glare from Rhys, he quickly changed his tune. "Fine," he sighed. "I'll be the best damn student you've ever had."

"That's more like it," Rhys praised as he teasingly ruffled Everett's hair, earning a pout. "Well, let's get on with our first lesson, then. How do you feel about learning how to use the bow today? I thought that might be the easiest thing for your leg, since learning to track—and other shit—requires a lot of walking."

"Will I actually be able to shoot things?" Everett asked with wide eyes.

"How else are you going to learn? I mean, no animals today, of course, but I have some old targets we can get started on."

Rhys pulled out the four heavy wooden targets from his backpack. Last winter, to keep his skill up to par, he'd spent many of his boring days shooting arrows out of the window to where he'd hung targets on the trees. All of the practice had left the targets riddled with holes and notches. They hadn't been touched in months, but now, they'd finally be put to good use again.

"Today, let's focus on aim rather than distance," Rhys said as he hung them from low branches. "Most of the time in actual hunting situations, you'll be shooting from pretty close anyway. I don't know if you've ever shot a gun before, but arrows have a much shorter range. I'd say no more than fifty yards away for me. That's why learning how to mask your scent, build a blind or perch, and even using prey animal call replicators or bait are just as important skills as learning to shoot."

Everett was quiet behind him for a moment before he spoke in a deadpan tone: "I have no fucking idea what you just said."

"Sorry, sorry—my bad. I forgot you don't know jack shit about hunting terms. Don't worry; I'll teach those to you, too, sometime," Rhys said with a chuckle.

He'd finished setting up the targets, so he turned his attention to his student, handing him one of his more basic compound bows and the accompanying arrows. "It's okay if you accidentally break this one, by the way—I have tons more, and I haven't even used this one since I moved out here."

"I like how you assume I'm going to break it. You have *so* much confidence in me, huh?" Everett scoffed. He turned the bow over in his hands a few times, admiring the sleek camouflage metal that matched their outfits.

"I mean, you have broken a lot of things since you've been here," Rhys said, putting a hand on his hip. "So, what do you think? How does it feel in your hands?"

Everett frowned, thumbing the bowstring like a guitar. "Good, I guess? Is it supposed to feel a certain way?"

Rhys shrugged. "Kinda? It should feel like it's the right weight and shape for your hands. Like you have a good, steady grip on it. Here, try pulling back the string a bit and tell me how it feels."

With Rhys's guidance, Everett tentatively pulled the bowstring until it couldn't go any farther—until his arms shook at the sheer effort it took to hold it in position.

"I-it's fine," he said through gritted teeth, clearly *not* fine, and Rhys couldn't help the giggle that burst out of his chest.

"Okay, maybe we are gonna need to adjust those settings a bit. Sorry, rookie. I think it still has the same settings on that I used when I tested it in the shop. But good on you for being able to at least pull it all of the way back."

Everett sighed in relief when he handed the bow back to Rhys. "This is way harder than I thought it would be. You're making me feel like a weakling."

"Don't feel bad about it," Rhys consoled as he whipped out his handy screwdriver to tinker with the settings. "I've been doing this for years. If you keep at this, I'm sure you'll be able to build enough strength and skill someday—ah, I think this should be better now. Okay, here, try it again."

This time, when Everett pulled the bowstring back, his arms stayed steady and strong, able to hold the position without major discomfort for a good few minutes. He looked up at Rhys with a wide, prideful smile. "Look! Look, I'm doing it!"

"Hell yeah, you are!" Rhys cheered, patting him on the back. "You're not going to be able to get as much power in the shot with these lower settings, but as long as you can aim properly to shoot right through the heart or lungs, it'll be enough."

For the next few minutes, Rhys demonstrated how to nock the arrow into the bow, explaining how crucial it was to make sure the arrow was secure before pulling the string back. Doing so with a loose arrow would have caused it to fall out and potentially scare away flighty prey. Everett listened with rapt attention, nodding along to the words though probably not understanding much of the hunting jargon. Thankfully, it seemed he was honoring his promise from earlier to be a good student, even asking clarifying questions that revealed minor yet important details Rhys hadn't thought to go over.

Frankly, being able to handle a compound bow wasn't the biggest achievement in the world—hell, some *children* could—but to Rhys, it felt as significant as successfully climbing Mount Everest when Everett confidently nocked an arrow all by himself. When he pulled it back, his hands were steady, making him look as much a seasoned pro as Rhys. He wondered in the back of his mind if this was how teachers felt when their students understood and actually cared about the knowledge passed on to them.

Though, when it was finally time for Everett to take his very first shot, the feeling was replaced with undeniable nerves. Holding his breath with his fingers crossed behind him, Rhys prayed Everett would at least be able to hit the outer portion of the target, knowing that not doing so could easily shatter his student's confidence—

"*Holy shit!*"

It didn't miss. Instead, the arrow pierced through the red dot in the center of the target, leaving Rhys's jaw dropping, and Everett letting out a high-pitched yelp. He dropped the bow and ran over to Rhys to engulf him in a suffocating bear hug.

"Oh my fucking god! Rhys! Did you see that? Did you fucking *see that*?" Everett yelled in his ear. "It went all the way through! Damn, Rhys, I thought you said those lower settings would be weak, but *fuck*! I hit the middle circle thingy! Can you believe it?"

"A *bullseye*," Rhys whispered, looking in awe at the target over Everett's shoulder. The arrow was still there, proof that it had, in fact, actually happened. For months, when Rhys had first been learning the ways of the bow, he hadn't hit a single bullseye. And yet, Everett had done it as though it was the simplest thing in the world.

"I told you I'd be the best student you've ever had." Everett grinned smugly, pulling back. "Are you proud of me?"

"Are you *really* asking me that?" Rhys shook his head before looking up at Everett with a smile. "Of course I am. Fuck, more than just proud. Everett, are you sure you've never used a bow before?"

"Nope," he replied. "Never ever in my life, I swear."

Rhys shook his head again in disbelief. "You really are something else."

★

At first, Rhys considered it beginner's luck—and maybe the fact that he had been such a thorough teacher—that Everett had managed to hit a bullseye on his first try.

But when the days of bow training flew by and his student still hadn't missed a single shot—not even when Rhys introduced greater distances and obstacles in the way—it had become quite obvious that Everett's raw talent deserved far beyond the simple excuse of beginner's luck.

A prodigy, Rhys called him, and rightly so.

With nothing much else to teach Everett about using a compound bow, Rhys decided to move his student onto the next aspect of hunting within a week rather than the three he had originally planned. Though, much to Rhys's immense disappointment, Everett wasn't exactly a well-rounded prodigy.

"I *hate* this," Everett complained with a huff. "I

thought you said that this was going to be easy! I'm so bored, and it's so cold! Why are we out here in the rain for so long?"

"Well, how was I supposed to know that you have the patience of an absolute *child*?" Rhys whisper-yelled, giving a sharp elbow to Everett's side that had him letting out a pained yelp. "We've literally only been sitting here for less than an hour, Everett. That's barely any time at all. Almost all of my hunts have me camping out for days before I even see a glimpse of a deer, so you better get used to it. And it's barely raining, which we can't even feel because of the trees."

"But why do we need to wait for the deer to come to us? Why can't we just go, I don't know, track one down? Wouldn't that be easier? I'm not even learning anything; we're just sitting here."

Rhys rubbed at his temples. Even though it wasn't even noon yet, he was beginning to feel a wicked headache brewing.

"Listen here," he said. "I know you think you're hot shit after shooting all of those bullseyes, but just that doesn't make a good hunter. Patience does. And that's what I'm teaching you today. How to be quiet, how to make a blind, how to camouflage, how to use bait, and how to be *fucking patient*."

"Oh, whatever." Everett scoffed. "Patience *shmatience*. That wasn't even an answer to my question. Why can't we just track the deer?"

"You're being such a brat right now, you know?" Rhys grumbled. "Yes, sometimes it can be easier to track down prey rather than wait for them. But, since it's getting close to winter, they're trying to eat as much as possible. So, they're harder to track and easier to lure when they're moving around so much. Hence, the apples."

Rhys gestured to the large pile of apples set out beyond their bush blind, glistening with raindrops. "Just trust me, okay? I know what I'm doing."

"Trust *shmust*."

"Oh my *god*, stop doing that!" Rhys groaned, throwing his head back. "Can you please stop arguing with me and be quiet? You're probably scaring all of the deer away, and I can't focus with you blabbing!"

Everett huffed and crossed his arms over his chest. "I don't smell any deer, but whatever. I'll shut up."

He stayed quiet for almost a good two hours of precious silence, leaning back against the tree and doodling in the mud with a stick. It reminded Rhys of himself as a child—forced to spend hours listening to the preacher babble at church every single Sunday, a quite boring affair that had been barely alleviated by him sketching all over his children's copy of the Bible. So, he understood. His mother had always been so immersed in the service, just as he was with the forest, attuned perfectly to every sound, scent, and movement.

Although there was no way he would even think about packing up early for Everett's sake, he still felt a twinge of pity for him.

But thankfully, Everett wouldn't have to wait much longer. Around sixty yards in the distance, Rhys caught the slight movement of the tree branches and the soft snap of hooves stepping on a stick. Somewhere out there, a deer stood hidden behind the thick foliage, seemingly deciding whether or not to take the risk to step into the small clearing where the pile of enticing apples lay.

Rhys narrowed his eyes, trying to make out the shape of its body, which wasn't an easy task since the dark clouds didn't leave enough light to contrast fur from leaves. Combined with the distance, there was no way he'd be able to make a good shot. He needed the deer to emerge in order to aim correctly for its vital organs, or even hit it at all. Which meant they'd have to be absolutely silent for it to feel safe enough to do so.

Nerves buzzed underneath Rhys's skin as he remembered how important this kill was. They might not get another chance like this one, not if winter came early. He tried his best to take in deep, long breaths, hoping his hands would stay steady. He could do this. The deer just needed to take a few more steps, and he would be golden.

"Hey, Rhys," Everett stage-whispered, shaking him by the shoulders. "Can we take a lunch break?"

Out of the corner of his eye, Rhys regarded him with a glare. Couldn't Everett see he was trying to focus? That there was a deer right in front of them?

"Not right now," Rhys hissed as quietly as possible, raising his finger to his mouth and making a *shh* sound.

He trained his eyes on the area again, watching as the deer barely poked its head out from behind a tree to scan the area. It was only a doe, no giant buck as he'd hoped. He normally didn't shoot does, but he was desperate, and this one was old and large enough that he had no qualms about it; she must have gone through multiple fawning seasons already.

Carefully, he lifted his crossbow and slowly nocked in an arrow. Any second now, she would step farther into view, and then he would be able to line up his shot.

"But I'm so hungry; we had breakfast, like, five hours ago," Everett whined. "Oh, wait, didn't you pack some rabbit jerky in your bag?"

Rhys's body, and the doe's, tensed as still as statues at the sound of Everett talking and unzipping his backpack.

"Everett, don't you fucking *dare—*"

"Relax, I won't make you look for it. You just keep staring at those apples, and I'll eat; don't worry! Now, where is that little baggie... Ugh, Rhys, why is there so much damn stuff in here? It's like you packed everything in the cabin."

As Everett rifled through the bag, all of the tools inside clanged against one another and bags of medical supplies crinkled, creating a symphony of chaos that had the doe taking a step back to hide behind the tree again. Rhys's breath picked up at the worry that she was about to bolt. He really, *really* wanted to curse and smack the shit out of Everett, but that would only cause the doe to be even more fearful.

Combined with the pitter-patter of rain, all of the noises affected his own anxiety as well. He couldn't focus on calming himself down when all he could think about was his anger at Everett, the pressure of needing to aim perfectly, his own hunger, the exhaustion from sitting out there for hours, the fear that the doe would run away, the fear of starving, and all of those *fucking noises*. It was too much, way too much for him to handle, making him so anxious his vision blurred and his hands shook as he pulled back the bowstring.

"Rhys, I can't find it—"

His complaining was cut off by the sound of the doe kicking at the foliage and the *whirr* of a desperate arrow shooting at nothing and only succeeding in impaling a tree.

"God*damn it*!" Rhys screamed as he fell onto his ass, tugging at his hair violently. "I could've had that! *Fuck*!

"Wait, was that *actually* a deer?" Everett asked with eyes widened in disbelief. His gaze flickered back and forth between the forest and Rhys, who had begun to rock back and forth and hyperventilate. "Oh shit... Rh-Rhys, um, hey, a-are you okay?"

Rhys didn't—couldn't—respond to him verbally. He couldn't even hear the words, not with the loud ringing in his ears. He tried his best to remember the coping strategies he'd learned years ago from his therapist, but he couldn't get his breathing under control, which only added to his panic. *Panic.* He was having a fucking panic attack, something he'd only experienced a couple of times since he'd moved to the forest. He thought he had been getting better, but no. No, he hadn't, at all. He was the same old Rhys who couldn't handle his emotions. He could never escape, no matter how hard he tried.

A hand gingerly touched his shoulder, warm and familiar. Words were being spoken at him in a voice just as familiar. He tried his best to latch on to the sensations, to ground himself in reality, yet he was already much too overwhelmed with the world swirling around him to be able to. He could only sit there in the pouring rain, shivering and covered in mud, forced to endure and wait out the storm raging inside him for what felt like hours of torture until he could finally shove the touch away, his body unable to sustain the panic state any longer.

"G-get off me!" Rhys exclaimed. "Don't f-fucking touch me!"

Everett let out an *oof* as he fell into the mud, splashing it all over the both of them. "Rhys, what—I was just trying to help you!"

"Help me? *Help me*? Really?" Rhys scoffed as he stumbled onto trembling, weak legs. "Fuck you, Everett, you weren't helping me at all!"

Everett blinked. "I...wasn't? But I thought the touching was helping you calm down—"

"You're the damn reason I was panicking in the first place! And now the reason we are going to starve because you couldn't just listen to me for one second!"

"I-I—" Everett shrank under Rhys's sharp glare as if pinned to the spot. "I'm sorry?"

"'Sorry' doesn't cut it," Rhys snapped.

He didn't like the frightened look on Everett's face—didn't like that *he* was the cause of it—but the anger and frustration that bubbled inside of him was hard to ignore, hard to suppress. In his rage, he picked up his bow from the ground, snapping one of his arrows in the process.

"Now this spot is ruined. No deer will come back here. And this day is ruined too. Goddamn it!"

In the cold autumn air, Rhys's heavy breaths puffed from his nose like torrents of smoke from an angry dragon. And even though he was almost a whole head shorter than Everett, in his rage, he seemed to tower over the poor man. Everett couldn't even meet Rhys's sharp eyes as he cowered in clear shame and guilt.

"I'm sorry, Rhys" was all Everett managed to say, yet again, his voice warbling as if he was seconds away from crying and rolling over onto his back to present his stomach like a dog.

"Stop fucking saying that," Rhys snarled.

He grabbed his bow, and Everett's, shoved them violently into his bag, and left the broken arrow lying pathetically in the mud—a complete waste of an arrow he had crafted so perfectly.

"'Sorry' doesn't put food on the table. You better not fucking complain about dinner tonight because I swear to god if you even *dare* to after today—" He cut himself off with a shake of his head. "Come on; let's go on home now. We have other shit to take care of."

Rhys didn't give Everett a chance to reply nor gather all of his things before he started trudging back toward the cabin. He walked so quickly Everett could barely keep up, limping behind him.

Chapter Four

Dinner that night was a tense affair.

The two hunters—*failed* hunters—were both starving after a very long, trying day. Yet, after they had scraped their bowls clean of fish stew, their bellies still rumbled quite loudly. Technically, there'd been enough for them to gorge themselves on, but without the safety net of the deer he'd hoped to bring back today, Rhys had to enforce the rationing policy, lest they die of starvation halfway through the upcoming winter. He had expected some sort of complaint from the ever-hungry Everett when he set down a half-full bowl. But after the events of earlier that day, the brat seemed to have diminished into a shell of the energetic, needy man he'd been only hours prior.

Not a single word had been spoken over their meal, the sounds of Everett's slurping and Rhys's spoon clinking against the wooden bowl echoing in the small cabin. Everett winced every time he made a bit of noise and looked guiltily at Rhys as if deathly afraid of being reprimanded again.

"Here, I-I'll take care of the dishes tonight" were the first rushed-out words Everett said all evening as he took the bowl from Rhys. Though, before Rhys could thank him, Everett had already scurried away to the sink in the blink of an eye.

Rhys was still angry, rage and disappointment simmering low in his stomach. In the last few hours, he'd had time to calm himself enough to a see he'd majorly fucked up, just as much as Everett. Sure, Everett had messed up the hunt, but Rhys had been way out of bounds for throwing what was, basically, a temper tantrum like a child denied his dessert. It wouldn't bring the deer back, after all, and had probably scared even more potential prey away from the area.

He loathed the look on Everett's face, how he walked on eggshells in order to not set Rhys off again and seemed as if he was about to grovel for his forgiveness. Rhys had never been good at apologizing, so it took two whole hours into the night before he finally decided to cut through the thick tension in the air.

"Everett," Rhys started. His gravelly voice startled the man seated with him—yet quite far apart from him—in front of the roaring fireplace.

"Y-yeah? Do you need something?"

And that hurt too—that Everett automatically defaulted to being, in a way, Rhys's obedient slave.

"That's— *No*, I don't need something." Rhys shook his head, gazing straight into the flames. "I wanted to apologize. For earlier, for how I acted. I didn't... I shouldn't have yelled at you. I didn't mean to scare you? Yeah. You don't have to forgive me, but just know that I... I don't know. I feel bad about it. I thought I had better control over myself than that. I shouldn't have taken my anxiousness out on you. But please don't be scared of me, not like everyone else. *Please.*"

The awful, rambling attempt at an apology had Rhys cringing inwardly. But thankfully, it caused Everett to finally look up from the floor, no longer sulking like a kicked puppy.

"It's okay," Everett replied in a small voice. "I shouldn't have been loud. I'm the one who should feel bad. I ruined a perfectly good hunt, and now because of me, we are going to *starve*."

"Hey, hey, we aren't going to starve. Don't listen to anything I said earlier, okay? I know I said we were gonna starve, but that was just me catastrophizing." Rhys reached out to place a soothing hand on Everett's shoulder. "It's not the end of the world; I promise. We can...we can go hunting tomorrow. It shouldn't be snowing for a few more weeks at least, maybe even another month. We have time. You just gotta be quieter next time? And it'll be all good."

Everett gnawed on his bottom lip. "Is that going to be enough time? It looks like it's going to snow..." His nostrils flared. "Very soon. Tomorrow, even."

Rhys raised his eyebrows. "Tomorrow? Why do you think that? It's raining right now, so it's not cold enough yet to actually snow. We should still have a few weeks."

Everett cocked his head to the side in confusion. "Because it smells like it's going to?"

"It *smells* like it's going to," Rhys parroted in a deadpan voice, narrowing his eyes. "How the fuck do you smell if it's going to snow or not?"

"Do you...not? I thought everyone could."

"No, I don't think everyone can." Rhys chuckled lightly at Everett's frown. "I don't think your magic sense of smell is quite right though. I've been out here long enough I'm pretty sure I can predict the weather weeks in advance. Anyway, it'll be fine. You're fine. But...are *we* okay? Because I don't want to make you scared like this ever again."

"I just..." Everett paused to sigh. "I just think...maybe I shouldn't be hunting with you anymore. Or staying here, even, since I'm becoming such a burden—"

"No!" Rhys exclaimed much too loudly, startling them both. He visibly cringed this time. "No," he said again, much quieter. "No, you are *not* a burden. Absolutely not. You do need to work on your patience, but otherwise, you're going to become a very good hunter, Everett. And I want you here."

"You want me here?" Everett whispered in disbelief. "*Why*? All I do is annoy you and make things harder for you. I haven't helped you out at all like I promised."

Rhys didn't know how to reply. The cabin filled with a pregnant silence as he thought to himself. Why *did* he want Everett to stay? It wasn't as if he brought much to the table that benefitted Rhys. All the guy really had going for him was that he had a knack for using a bow and, apparently, could smell future weather changes. And, if Rhys was honest, Everett whispering him soothing words and stroking his back during his panic attack had helped ground him back to reality somewhat. Everett may have been the cause, but he was so understanding and sweet. He was also one hell of a good space heater and pillow to sleep with at night as well as an entertaining conversationalist. Rhys hadn't ever realized he'd been greatly missing someone like him until Everett had barged his way into his life. Someone he didn't want to lose.

He knew Everett would leave someday, whether it was bright and early tomorrow morning or months in the future. No matter how long he stayed, Rhys could foresee missing the brat, reaching out for his long-gone warmth during the nights, and sitting in the lonesome silence of the cabin until his brain began to hallucinate hearing voices.

"It's...because I'm lonely, I guess" was what Rhys ended up saying as he nervously scratched the back of his neck, avoiding Everett's gaze, which felt as if it was looking straight through him.

"Lonely? But I thought you liked being alone? I was worried I've been ruining that for you."

"Honestly? I thought you'd ruin it, too, at first. But I think, in a way, having you here only made me realize how *alone* I was. How much I missed company despite too much company being the very reason I'm even up here. Yeah, you annoy the absolute shit out of me sometimes, but I'd rather be annoyed than lonely. If that makes sense? I don't know if it does, but like—"

Before Rhys could finish his embarrassing rambling, his words were cut short by Everett suddenly enveloping him in yet another overly tight hug, pressing his face into the soft cotton of the borrowed sweater.

"You want me here," Everett singsonged as he rocked the two of them back and forth, voice giddy and lacking all signs of the nervousness of only minutes prior. "You want me here, and you like me!"

"I never said I *like* you," Rhys mumbled.

"No, but you wouldn't want me here if you didn't." Everett giggled as he pulled back, still holding Rhys in his arms. He reached out to boop his nose, making Rhys's face scrunch up. "You can't fool me! Ah, and all of this time I thought you hated me or something. This is such a *relief*. I was worried for a second that you'd kick me out into the cold."

"Do you really think I'm that heartless? I'm wounded, Everett!"

Though Rhys was feigning offense with his gasp, it seemed Everett hadn't caught on to the joke, his giggles fading out and smile faltering.

"No, Rhys, you're far from heartless," he said softly as he pulled back completely as if to give Rhys space. "Just...thought I fucked up enough to deserve it. Especially after all you've done for me."

"Aw, come on, it isn't that big of a deal." Rhys's face heated up at the words, and he was unable to look up. "Anyone else would do the same thing. Leaving you there would be like leaving you to *die*. I don't think any sane person would do that. I was just doing the right thing."

"Yeah, but I doubt everyone would go the extra mile like you've been doing. Not only saving me, but letting me into your home, teaching me how to hunt. You don't need to do those things for me but...you are, and I think that says a lot about you. How nice you are."

"Oh, stop it. I'm far from a saint. You have no idea the things I've done in the past, Everett. You wouldn't think that if you knew. You're not the first person I've taken my anger out on."

"That doesn't count, so try me with something else," Everett replied without hesitation. "Tell me all of these awful things Big Bad Rhys has done, and we'll see if your words hold true. I can bet you, though, nothing can phase me."

"'Big Bad Rhys'?" He shook his head with a smile. "I guess that's a fitting title."

"Come on; no changing the subject." Everett grabbed Rhys's forearm and shook it impatiently. "Tell me."

"You aren't going to shut up about this, are you? Even after all this talk about being more quiet? More *patient*?"

"We aren't hunting right now, so…I should be allowed to talk all I want. And you are allowed to, too, so spill the beans, Rhys. I want to hear all of your stories! I bet they're really cool—ooh, were you a rogue or something sick like that? Did you *kill* anyone? Is that why you are out here all alone?" Everett gasped dramatically.

Rhys let out a huff of laughter. "You're way too excited about me being some dangerous criminal or whatever you seem to think I am."

"Then what is it? I'm dying here, Rhys, *dying*!" Everett shook his arm again. "Why are you even out here, anyway, if you aren't in trouble for killing someone? Oh, wait, I got it!

"You're out here because you tried to steal someone's mate, huh? Wow, what a Casanova you are." He whistled, impressed. "Good with the ladies, aren't you? Makes sense with that pretty face of yours. You need to teach me your ways with that, too— Well, maybe not, since you were obviously unsuccessful."

"*Pretty*— Wait, wait, someone's mate? What the fuck? Everett, I'm not running from anything, and I'm not wanted for any crimes or for trying to ruin someone's marriage. My life isn't some shit straight out of a television show."

"Uh, okay...but I thought you said you've done bad things. What else could that mean?"

Rhys cleared his throat. "Just...I've hurt a lot of people, leaving them behind to live out here. Cutting them out of my life even though they cared about me. Taking my anger out on them; I've literally given people black eyes before. And..."

Rhys looked pointedly down at the bandages still wrapped tightly around Everett's leg. "*That* is my fault. The trap you got yourself stuck in? Yeah, that was me. I set that trap. Not to hurt you intentionally, of course—I put a few out to capture and kill a wolf that's been bugging the shit outta me lately, stealing all of my food. I don't think that's something a good person would do."

Just thinking about the wolf, even now, a few weeks since the last time he'd been graced with its dreaded presence, Rhys felt the usual twinge of annoyance and frustration—and a bit of hunger—at the reminder of all of the meals he'd lost to the paws of the sneaky predator.

"A-a *wolf*? Like you told me about?" Everett whispered, his eyes darting around nervously, his skin a bit pale as if he feared the wolf would pop out from behind the bookshelves and rip them to pieces.

"Yeah, *that* wolf." Rhys leaned in close to rest a comforting hand on Everett's shoulder. He didn't blame him for fearing the sharp-toothed, hungry predator that lurked somewhere in the woods. Hell, even Rhys would be terrified if he were to come across it unarmed. "But don't worry; it won't hurt you. I've been carrying my gun around with me recently, so if it does come around, I'll be ready to take care of it, okay? You don't need to be afraid."

"Would you..." Everett paused to gulp heavily, his Adam's apple bobbing. "Sh-shoot it? Kill it?"

Though Everett seemed afraid of the wolf, it was just as clear that watching it be riddled with bullet holes wasn't something he'd want to witness. And, well, neither would Rhys, but—

"If I had to, yes," Rhys said. "I was going to kill it, if I hadn't ended up catching you in the trap instead. But maybe warning shots will be enough to scare it away, so I wouldn't have to. I'd rather avoid killing it, to be honest. I feel bad for setting those traps out; it was a rash decision."

Everett nodded enthusiastically. "Yeah. B-Because life is precious, right?" he blurted out much too loudly for the small space. "There's...uh, there's no need to waste the wolf's life, for no reason, r-right?"

"Well, I mean, there's *technically* a reason," Rhys grumbled. "But, yeah, I'm not one of those damn trophy hunters who hunt for sport. That shit is sick. I only kill for necessity, like for food or safety— Hey, Everett, are you all right?"

"Wh-what—*oh*." Everett laughed nervously, looking down at his hands with wide eyes as if he hadn't even realized they were shaking. He shifted his gaze back to Rhys, whose concerned expression only seemed to make Everett even more pale. "I-I'm fine, I'm okay. Sorry, I just don't like talking about death all that much."

"That's completely understandable. Let's talk about something else, then, yeah?" Rhys offered without hesitation, to which Everett responded with a nod and a small, relieved smile.

Rhys hummed thoughtfully for a moment before continuing. "How about... Hmm, didn't you want to know why I live out here by myself? It's a long story, but if you really wanna hear it, I don't mind telling it."

It was the right thing to say, thankfully, if Everett's eyes lighting up and sparkling with interest was enough to go by.

"Will you?" Everett asked hopefully. "I mean, don't feel pressured to or anything, but—"

"Oh shush. I'm not feeling pressured. I want to tell you, you dork. I was just teasing you before. You were coming up with some pretty outlandish theories— I *wish* the reality was just as interesting. I hope I don't disappoint you by saying my story is...much lamer. Long, but lame. If you fall asleep in the middle of it, don't worry, it's fine."

Everett rolled his eyes. "I doubt it's lame. I'll be the judge of that."

"I'm sure you will," Rhys said with a sigh.

They moved to lie down side by side on the bed, staring up at the ceiling, studying the grains and knots in the wooden planks as if they were stars.

"So...I've never told anyone in detail about my mental illnesses, except for my therapist, and it's been way too long since I've seen her, not since high school. I have what's called sensory processing disorder, as well as agoraphobia, depression, anxiety... I'm a disaster, really.

"It's hard to explain, but that's why I had that panic attack earlier. All of the sounds combined with the fear and anger... It was just too many senses at once, overwhelming me and turning me into that absolute mess of a person. It's something I don't really understand myself...but it dictates my entire life, pretty much. It's the reason I moved out here, away from the city. I had panic attacks like that multiple times a day."

"You used to live in the city?" Everett asked. "Ah, I've seen them from afar before, but I've never been in one. They look so cool, all lit up and sparkly—oh wait—that sounds like it wouldn't be fun for you."

Rhys snorted. "Yeah, it's pretty from 'afar,' but living in it fucking sucks. Even the damn suburbs are too much for me. All of the people, cars, busses, streetlights, stores, smells... I hated it there. The city isn't really anything to idolize, Everett... Well, maybe you'd like it, actually. I'm the only person I know who's so negatively affected by it. It sounds so stupid, I know—"

"It isn't. It's definitely not stupid; don't say that! I doubt you're the only one, and to be honest, I don't think I'd like it that much either."

"Oh, yeah, 'cuz of your sensitive nose, huh? That would be pretty overwhelming for you. The city smells like burning garbage." Rhys chuckled, scrunching up his nose at the thought. "Well, I guess it's nice to know you understand somewhat. My entire life there was spent feeling like a weirdo, an outsider. I had some friends, but nobody understood, not even my own damn family. Fuck, my parents would get so mad at me when they'd have to pick me up from school because I'd have a panic attack, or when I was older and they'd get calls that I was skipping classes again for the same reason. It was the worst when I'd have one in public—which was like all of the damn time. Especially in grocery stores when my dad would drag me outside and tell me 'It's a grocery store. Stop fucking crying or I'll give you something to actually cry about.'"

Everett's hand—when had they started holding hands? Rhys didn't remember—squeezed his own. "Did they ever...hurt you?"

"No," Rhys whispered with a sigh. "No, but it was just as bad... Them yelling at me would just send me into another panic attack. So damn counterintuitive. You'd think if they wanted me to stop, they'd stop yelling, right? Ha, honestly, I was kind of relieved when they kicked me out. I didn't have to deal with seeing their pissed off, disappointed faces any longer.

"But...living on my own in the city wasn't easy. I couldn't afford psychiatric care any longer without their insurance. Thankfully, they had transferred my college fund a few years prior, so I was able to try to move on with my life, to go to college...and of course, that didn't go very well. It was somehow even worse than grade school because at least then, the material didn't matter much, so I could listen to music and read a book. In college, though, I had to pay attention, or else I'd fail. How the fuck did anyone manage to pay attention in a lecture hall full of people whispering under the sound of the professor's voice booming, with all their disgusting smelling colognes and perfumes, and with the fluorescent lights that were overly bright?"

"Your...um...school sounds awful." Everett frowned. "What's cologne and perfume?"

"Stuff people spray on their bodies to smell good, usually really strong. Fruits and flowers and shit. I dunno. I never wore any."

"That sounds disgusting. Why would anyone wanna smell like a flower? A person's natural scent is perfect the way it is."

"I guess...but it really was disgusting. All that shit made me end up failing every single class I tried. After a year, I ran out of money, so I had to get a job in order to pay my rent for the bed in the local youth hostel. Since I had no degree, I was forced to work in low-end, minimum wage, customer-service jobs—all ten of which ended in me being fired for crying in front of the customers. My record was three weeks." Rhys laughed darkly, humorlessly. "Have you ever worked a retail job like that before?"

Everett was quiet for a moment before answering. "No, I've never had a job before."

"You lucky ass," Rhys grumbled, though not in anger. "They suck, all of them. After number ten, I was just so fucking done. I didn't want to try again, because I knew I would fail again, and again, and again. So, with no prospects left, nothing to my name but a meagre savings account, I decided to just fuck everything! Fuck living in the city! I didn't care anymore, not even when my few friends tried to convince me to stay. They offered me rooms in their places, offered me job connections, but I knew I couldn't be happy in the city at all. My decision ruined those friendships... I hurt their feelings so much by saying they couldn't make me happy. But it was the truth. I had to leave. And so...I moved out here."

Rhys's frown morphed into a small smile as he remembered the day he first stepped foot on his property, where the only sounds were that of the wind rustling through the trees and birds chirping in their nests. He knew immediately that here was where he was meant to be. The forested mountains had always been his home, had always called out for him in their own perfectly silent way, even before he'd thought about moving to them. It had been worth leaving everything and everyone behind. He was content, for the first time in his life.

"I'm really sorry you had to go through that, but you're not evil for chasing after what makes you happy. I know you probably miss them though."

Rhys shrugged. "Eh, sometimes. But I think I prefer you as a friend over them."

Everett let out a squeal that had Rhys chuckling. "I'm a better friend?"

"Of course you are; are you kidding? Nobody else has been this...patient and understanding with my annoying ass."

"Oh, shush, I'm the annoying one here, you said so yourself!"

"Different kind of annoying. You're childish, and I'm an asshole. Anyway, moving on!" Rhys said, cutting Everett off before he could argue further. "I built this whole place myself, including digging out my underground food cellar." He motioned to the hatch on the floor in the kitchen.

"*Really?*" Everett gasped. He looked around the small cabin, eyes wide and clearly impressed. "How'd you do that?"

"Eh, it took a long time, but it wasn't too hard," Rhys explained, stroking the wooden planks of the floor lovingly. "My life savings went to buying the property and a nice tent to live in for the first summer. All of the materials to build, all of the furniture, and everything else was bought by selling the things I'd hunt—you'd be surprised how much a deer can buy you. The books over there I brought with me though."

He gestured to the bookshelves lining the wall opposite of the fireplace, all hand-built and full to the brim with books in various conditions. Some were brand new and never touched, and others looked like they could be older than Rhys himself, falling apart at the bindings. From encyclopedias to romance novels, he had it all.

"Wow, Rhys." Everett whistled. "I didn't notice how many you had until now. Have you actually read them all?"

Rhys gave a small smile. "Not all of them, but most of them, some even hundreds of times. Don't make fun of me, but...the *Harry Potter* books are my favorite."

"*Harry Potter*...am I supposed to know what that is?"

"You—*what*?" Rhys couldn't believe what he was hearing, his mouth gaped open like a fish. "You've never read any before? Never even *heard* of it? What the fuck, were you raised in the woods or something? Under a rock? In a cave?"

"N-no, not a cave, of course not! Wh-why would you think that?" Everett exclaimed in a rush. "I wasn't raised in a cave. I was raised in a house just like you were, d-duh!"

"Uh...okay? Sure? I was joking, you dork." Rhys regarded him from the corner of his eye—the guy seemed embarrassed. Who could possibly not know about the *Harry Potter* series? "You should read them sometime though. I'll let you borrow them if you want. Could help pass the time when we eventually get snowed in, you know? 'Cuz that's what I'm gonna be doing pretty much the whole time."

"Um." Everett cleared his throat awkwardly. "No, thanks? I'm...not really much of a reader."

"Well, that's fine. Reading isn't for everyone. Honestly, school almost ruined it for me, being forced to read books I didn't give a single fuck about. All of those goddamn *useless* essays were a waste of my time and energy—" Rhys cut himself off with a shake of his head. Sitting them both up, he grabbed Everett's shoulders, looking him straight in the eyes. "Never go to college, Everett, never. It's a *scam*, no matter what your brainless high school advisors tell you. Promise me, okay?"

Everett nodded hesitantly. "Promise. But, it's not like I'd ever actually have the chance to even choose to go to college. Even if I wanted to, I don't think I could get in anyway..."

Rhys furrowed his brows. "Why not? Sure, you're a little too hyperactive to sit still in a lecture hall for hours, but you're a smart kid, Everett. Smart enough to get into at least some state college, if not better."

"You're going to think I'm weird if I tell you..." Everett mumbled, looking down at his lap.

"No, I won't. I promise."

Everett was silent for a long, tense moment, so long that for a second, Rhys began to worry he'd said something wrong. Obviously, Everett's homelife didn't really seem like something he was over the moon about discussing—Rhys hoped he hadn't accidentally triggered some horrible memory in the poor guy's brain. After all, he *had* said he was running from something. He was about to change the subject when Everett finally replied.

"I'm..." Everett started, then stopped again, as if unsure of how to vocalize his thoughts. "I never went to school? Like, *actual* school, like you."

That wasn't exactly what Rhys was expecting him to say—but leagues better, to his relief.

"Oh, like homeschool, right?" he asked with a small, comforting smile. "That's not weird, plenty of kids are homeschooled. Actually, my childhood friend and next-door neighbor was homeschooled, and if my memory is right, I believe he managed to get a pretty sweet scholarship deal somewhere nice."

"Yeah, I guess you can call it that?" Everett replied. "But, uh...I was never taught to, erm, read, I guess? My family didn't think it was important to teach me."

That was more like Rhys had expected, making his smile fall into a frown. What kind of family didn't teach their son to read? It was no wonder Everett had no idea what *Harry Potter* was. Rhys wanted to ask more, wondered if Everett had been raised in some sort of awful cult, wanted to go find this "family" of his and give them a piece of his mind for withholding such an important life skill from Everett, but he held himself back.

"Well, damn, okay, you got me. That's weird—more like concerning, actually."

Everett pouted, crossing his arms over his chest. His cheeks were as red and warm as the scorching flames in the fireplace, gaze vehemently stuck anywhere but on Rhys. "I *told* you—"

"*But*," Rhys interrupted before Everett became even more upset. "That doesn't mean you can't learn *now*. I can teach you, you know. We're going to have a fuck ton of free time soon. I don't think it'll be as easy as learning how to hunt, of course, but I'm sure I can teach you the basics."

If it was even possible, Everett's face flushed darker, a view Rhys only got to see for a split second before it was hidden behind Everett's knees.

"Rhys," Everett whined, the sound muffled. "I can't ask you to do that, no! You've already done so much for me...*too* much."

"You're not asking— I'm offering; there's a difference." Rhys laughed. "Come on. It's really no big deal. We're gonna be stuck in this cabin for weeks or maybe even months, Everett. Honestly, you'd be doing *me* a favor by letting me teach you. It'd be fun. Much more entertaining than rereading the same books as last year a hundred more times."

"You're just saying that to be nice," Everett mumbled. "I doubt I'm even smart enough to spell my own name."

"That's—no, don't talk about yourself like that. Like I said, you're plenty smart. It's not your fault you weren't taught certain things." Rhys reached to put a hand on Everett's knee. "Look, we don't have to start today, tomorrow, or even this month. I just want you to think about it, okay?"

It was quiet for a few moments before Everett peeked over his knees, looking up at Rhys with red-rimmed eyes and slightly damp cheeks. "O-okay."

Rhys grinned encouragingly. "Good. Now, how do you feel about me reading to you from one of my books? Even if learning to read isn't something you're interested in, you can at least listen to others read aloud and still get the chance to experience these amazing stories. How does that sound, hmm? I'll even let you pick which one."

At that, Everett perked up a bit more, looking back to the bookcase again. "How...would I pick one? I can't read the titles..."

"Just pick whatever stands out to you. The cover art, I guess? And if you get bored or don't like your pick, you can choose a different one."

Thankfully intrigued, Everett stood up and headed over to pull out each and every book on the shelf with delicate hands, as if afraid he might break one of them. Rhys watched with a pleased expression—that fell into an annoyed sneer when he spotted what book Everett had decided on.

"You picked fucking *Twilight*, huh?" he grumbled, wishing he could glare burning holes through the glossy cover of the dreaded novel in Everett's hands. "I thought I had thrown that thing away."

"What's wrong with it? The apple looks pretty and tasty," Everett said as he sat back down. Rhys had been gifted the book by a friend in high school as a joke. He, of course, never read it.

Rhys scoffed. "Of course you picked it because it has a picture of food, you perpetually hungry monster. Trust me, the contents of this book aren't as good as the tasty-looking apple."

Everett whined. His dark eyes glittered in a big puppy-dog plea—one that, no matter how many times Everett pulled it on him, Rhys couldn't ever seem to be able to refuse. He could already feel himself giving in. It was completely unfair. No one should be allowed to wield so much power over another person with a simple face.

"You said I could choose any, Rhys." Everett snickered. "And I want you to read me this one. No backing out now!"

Rhys shook his head but relented in the end, taking the book and flipping it open to the first chapter.

Chapter Five

Somehow, it seemed Everett's magic nose powers proved to have been true. When they awoke the next morning, bright and early, to try their hand again at hunting, they opened the front door only to be met with the sight of a winter wonderland.

Around a foot of snow had fallen during the night, which would have been pretty in any other circumstance. It covered the entire landscape, leaving the tree branches bare of leaves and weighed down by piles of snow, and the ground an unblemished blanket of white. Though it was quite a beautiful sight to see, that didn't make it a welcome one.

"Out of all of the days, it just had to snow today. I swear, winter has it fucking out for me," Rhys grumbled as he dug through the coat closet, searching for the cleats that would strap onto their boots to give them better traction.

As Everett stepped out onto the porch, he gasped, looking around with wide, excited eyes. "Whoa, look at all that snow! Race you to the outhouse!"

"W-wait, Everett— You can't go outside without the cleats!" Rhys exclaimed, quickly standing up and hurrying outside. But he was too late to stop Everett, who was already a few yards ahead running through the snow, giggling all the way.

"Everett, stop right now. You're going to—"

Cringing, Rhys watched Everett do exactly what he was about to warn him about. As he lifted one foot in the air, the other lost its grip on the ground, causing him to tumble forward with an echoing shriek. Thankfully, he caught his balance before he landed smack onto his face, but in order to do so, he ended up falling into almost a perfect forward split.

"Ow, fuck!" Everett said with a hiss of pain as he scrambled to pull himself up into a sitting position.

Rhys cursed under his breath as he rushed to find the cleats, strapped a pair onto his boots, grabbed another pair, and hurried out to where Everett sat. He knelt beside him, looking at where Everett was clutching his injured leg with gritted teeth.

"Fuck, are you okay? Did you reopen the wound or something?" Rhys asked, scanning the leg for any signs of blood seeping through.

"N-no, I don't think so, but that stretch hurt. Really, really bad," Everett groaned.

Rhys let out a sigh of relief when he didn't see any red staining his pants. "At least you didn't fall backward and hit your head, but that still looked like it was pretty painful. A perfect split though! I bet you could be a gymnast prodigy, too, with that flexibility." He chuckled. "Anyway, I told you that you needed to put on the cleats, but *no*, you didn't listen to me, like usual! You can't just go running across ice without them! Here, strap these on before you break your head open."

Everett's brows furrowed as he did as he was told. "I know that, but I didn't see any ice. I thought it was all fluffy snow."

"On top, yes," Rhys said as he dug through the layer of freshly fallen snow and pushed it aside to reveal the layer of ice underneath. He knocked on it with his gloved fist; it sounded as solid as a hardwood door. "But it was raining yesterday, remember? That's where this dangerous shit came from. Since we live on level ground, the water didn't run down the hill. It sat here and froze overnight. That's why we always have to have the cleats on."

Everett peered down at the ice, checking out his distorted reflection. "The land around where, um, my family lived wasn't like this. It was all snow, no ice. We used to chase one another around for hours without falling—except for when we'd tackle one another, of course."

"That sounds like fun," Rhys said with a small smile, holding back the urge once again to ask more about this family of his. "But you can't do that here, okay? At least not without your cleats on. Here, how about you come inside and lie down for a while?"

"Eh, I think I'm okay out here," Everett said, lying down on his back and closing his eyes. "The cold feels really good on my legs."

"What, are you going to take a nap out here or something while I clear all of the snow by myself?"

"What, are you going to make an injured man shovel snow?" Everett asked, peering with one eye open and raising a brow with a sly smirk.

Rhys snorted and shook his head. "Touché. All right, smartass, fine. But don't start complaining when you get bored or freeze your ass off. And you better help me out once you feel better."

For the next hour, Rhys worked hard to clear the perimeter of the cabin and its roof as best he could with his shovel, sweating under layers of clothing from the effort despite the freezing cold nipping at every inch of exposed skin it could reach. It was a necessary evil, though, a task that needed to be done to keep the short path to the outhouse and the longer path to the river accessible, as well as the roof from caving in on them.

Rhys had learned his lesson the hard way during his first winter, when he had let the snow sit untouched for days. It had been only a foot, so he hadn't seen any need to clear it urgently—until one night, when so much snow had fallen that, combined with the previous snow, it completely blocked the doorway. Each time he had taken a stab at the gigantic mound with his shovel, more snow came rushing down to fill its place, causing him to be stuck in the cabin for almost two weeks, unable to even use the outhouse.

While it was possible for him to walk through the snow with the proper equipment, the weather still greatly inhibited his ability to hunt, since the deer would have already migrated down to the lower valleys where they had a better chance at finding food. Even if there were any deer still around, sitting all day in the cold sounded like hell frozen over to Rhys. The only prey he'd be able to catch were fish and rabbits, which he planned on doing every day.

It was in moments like these that Rhys regretted picking a property so high up on the mountain, cursing his past self for choosing it over one farther down into the valley—the thousand or so dollars he had saved in costs didn't seem worth it, in the end.

"I fucking hate this," Rhys groaned as he threw his shovel down and collapsed onto the porch to take a well-deserved break.

"Why do you hate winter so much? The snow is so much fun," Everett called out, his breath as white as the snow beneath him. He was still on his back, swishing his arms and legs to create what must have been his twentieth snow angel. "Come on, Rhys! Enjoy the snow with me!"

"Not all of us can play around in the damn snow all day, you know. You're lucky I'm too nice to force an injured man to do hard labor. Honestly, though, I'm unconvinced by your claims that your leg still hurts. It's been an hour since you fell. You should be fine enough now to help me out."

"I must've bruised it or something; I don't know."

"You couldn't have bruised it from the way you fell, since you didn't even hit the gr—*ow*! Everett, what the hell?"

Everett, the fucking menace, giggled wildly at Rhys's snow-covered face, a result of the snowball he'd chucked at him in retaliation—a surprisingly hard throw Rhys swore would give him a black eye.

"You little *brat*!" Rhys exclaimed, glaring at Everett as he swiped a gloved hand across his face. "You think this is so funny, don't you?"

"Y-you deserved it! For being m-mean." Everett managed to say between bursts of laughter. "Don't be such a stick in the mud. Come on, play with me!"

Rhys's frown grew into a smirk. If it was a snowball fight Everett wanted, well, Rhys would give him one.

"You wanna see me be mean?" he asked as he scooped up a snowball larger than his own head. "Game on."

Everett's eyes widened, and with a squeak, he jumped up and took off at light speed into the forest—Rhys was right; he'd definitely been lying about his leg still hurting—just in time to dodge the incoming attack.

Rhys knew it wasn't the best idea to be running around in the snow, especially after Everett's fall, but it was a *competition* now. There was no time to play it safe when his pride was on the line. No way could he lose a snowball fight to Everett of all people. So, Rhys pushed his fears to the back of his mind and ran after him.

Once he finally spotted Everett in the distance after what must have been a good ten minutes of chasing his ass down like a deer, Rhys created another snowball and mustered all his strength to chuck it at Everett's back. Though the force wasn't up to snuff with Everett's first throw, it had him yelping and rubbing at his back to Rhys's immense satisfaction.

"How do you like that, huh? What, can't take what you dish out?"

"N-no, you just startled me!"

Everett quickly scooped up another snowball and threw it at Rhys's face yet again. Rhys ducked in time, narrowly dodging the projectile.

"Pfft, you can do better than *that*," Rhys said with a laugh before he knelt to gather more snow. Everett shrieked at the sight, making Rhys laugh uncontrollably as he watched him back up skittishly, clearly about to take off.

Rhys wouldn't have that though. "Oh no you don't! Don't you run away from me!" he yelled as he surged forward, arm prepared to throw.

Except the ball never left his hand. Instead, the world slipped out from under him, his cleats unable to get enough traction on the ice hidden beneath the snow. Rhys fell backward, both feet in the air. For a moment, he swore he saw his life flash before his eyes as he plummeted to the ground in slow motion, cursing himself for running in these conditions. Why had he thought this would be a good idea? Now, he was certainly going to break a bone, or even split his head open on the hard ice, all because he wanted to win a fucking snowball fight.

But just before he hit the ground, only an inch away from impact, an arm caught him by his waist. For a moment, he thought he might have actually died after all and gone to heaven, staring up at the beautiful cloudy sky, head spinning, until he heard a voice calling out his name—a voice that begged him to look.

And so he did.

He expected to be greeted with the sight of God welcoming him to heaven, but who he actually saw was just as breathtaking. A person with a manly, sharp jawline that contrasted perfectly with full, pinkened cheeks. A person with equally plump lips, soft and begging to be kissed and somehow unaffected by the cold that should've made them chapped and dry. A person with two familiar, dark-brown, enchanting eyes, framed by long, thick eyelashes, which had caught specks of snowflakes. The eyes were wide, but not in the puppy-dog way Rhys was used to. They were *terrified*, scanning Rhys's body up and down.

"Rhys!" Everett exclaimed. His voice was so deep—had Rhys ever noticed that before? "A-are you okay? You almost broke your head open or something. Thank fuck I managed to catch you in time."

As he registered the words, Rhys realized the position he was in, cradled against Everett's chest like a baby, or maybe even a bride. He stared up at him as if hypnotized, admiring his facial features, which was nothing short of extremely embarrassing. Rhys's cheeks instantly turned red, and he moved a gloved hand up to hide them from view. What was wrong with him? Had he actually hit his head or something?

"I-I...I'm okay," he replied quietly, his voice cracking. "I...thank you, Everett. You just saved my life."

Everett sighed in relief as he pushed back the fringe from Rhys's face. "I'm so glad you're okay. You weren't wrong; the snow's dangerous. And I thought my little slip earlier was scary."

"W-will you let me get up now, please?" Rhys rasped.

"Uh...yeah. Yeah, totally, uh, sorry."

As if touching Rhys had burned him, Everett quickly helped him onto his feet and let go, then shoved his hands into the pockets of his jacket. Rhys averted his gaze as he dusted the snow off, cursing at himself internally for having been such a ditsy idiot—not only falling, but making the situation even weirder by creepily staring at Everett, scaring him in more ways than one. Out of the corner of his eye, he saw how Everett's body had shrunk in on itself slightly, as if he was afraid to be reprimanded—though Rhys hadn't said a word as they walked back to the cabin in silence.

Luckily, it wasn't a very long walk, only half a mile or so. Unfortunately, despite the short length, time seemed to slow down for the sole purpose of pointing out the awkwardness between them. Too many thoughts whirled like some twisted tornado in Rhys's mind, all centered around Everett.

He felt so ashamed for making Everett uncomfortable. All he'd done was save Rhys from cracking his head open and dying, not creating some sort of cringy Hallmark movie moment where the main characters realized their attraction toward each other. Yet, Rhys's adrenaline-fueled brain had gone there anyway. And now, when he glanced over at Everett as they walked, Rhys was reminded yet again of his attractiveness. Not only his face, but his large frame, his long legs that had moved fast enough to catch him before he hit the ground, his strong arms that held his weight for so long—

Rhys shook his head, trying to rid himself of the thoughts. What was he, thirteen years old again when he'd realized his attraction toward the same sex? What was *wrong* with him? This was wildly inappropriate. Everett was his friend, his student, not some man he'd met at a bar. Rhys didn't even know if he was gay or not. He knew very well from experience that any sort of attraction toward a friend—a *straight* friend—would surely end up in disaster. And this was one friendship Rhys definitely didn't want to taint and ruin. There was no way he would let himself be attracted to Everett. Sure, he was handsome, but it didn't mean a thing. Rhys didn't need to care, didn't need to make this more than it was.

He didn't care. He *didn't*.

"Rhys?"

He snapped his head up, thoughts falling aside like a discarded cloak, draping itself across the ground in heavy wrinkles.

"Y-yeah? What's up?" he mumbled, trying to appear normal with a strained smile.

"You...okay?" Everett asked, tilting his head to the side.

"Yeah, I think so." Rhys decided after another moment of quiet. "But I won't be if I have to stay here and freeze my ass off for much longer. Let's go inside, okay?"

Everett grinned. "You're right; sorry for stalling. Let's go warm up by the fire. Your lips are turning blue right now."

Unlocking the front door with a *click*, Rhys nodded eagerly. "Sounds like a great idea,"

He looked back over his shoulder for a moment, sighing when he saw how much snow he still needed to clear. He'd have to finish the chore soon and eventually go fish and set snares. But for now, all he wanted was to forget about what had happened and actually feel his fingers and toes again with the help of the fireplace.

He tried not to think about it as they ate dinner, his cheeks pinkening at Everett's slight groans of admiration at the food's flavor. He tried not to think about it when they lay down in bed together, Everett's body cocooning him in comfort and warmth. Thankfully, Everett didn't seem to feel uncomfortable any longer, holding him close as they did every night. To Rhys, however, it felt different, knowing an attractive man was spooning him with his butt pressed to his crotch.

Clearing his throat, Rhys decided he wouldn't allow his thoughts to snowball yet again—there were plenty of other more important things to worry about.

"So, the snow melts pretty slowly here in the mountains," he began, voice a bit rough from all of the yelling and laughter. "This will probably be gone in about a week, or at least mostly gone. Then, we'll be able to go hunting. But for now, we're going to have to conserve more and go catch fish and rabbits more often."

Everett nodded with a yawn. "Sounds good to me."

That deep, smooth baritone voice. Did his voice *have* to sound so damn hot? Couldn't he notice that Rhys was trying to ignore his annoyingly attractive qualities right now? The nerve!

"G-Good," Rhys mumbled, sounding and feeling flustered—which became worse when Everett, for some odd reason, decided to hold him closer, his hands wrapped securely around Rhys's waist.

Why did Rhys enjoy this so much? It must've been because of the warmth. He was merely using Everett as a space heater. It was mutually beneficial cuddling to keep themselves warm through the cold weather. Nothing more, nothing less. Absolutely nothing to overthink. Strictly platonic.

Chapter Six

Unfortunately, Rhys's estimation of the snow clearing within a week was far from accurate. The snow did begin to melt away slowly, which made the pair of hunters hopeful and itching to get back out into the forest. At the end of the week, Rhys planned for them to hunt the next day, since it should be clear enough. But winter had other ideas.

Rhys awoke at dawn to the sensation of a warm body pressed up against him. He jolted up and let out a groan. Sleepily leaning on Everett's tensed shoulder, he pressed a hand to his chest, trying to catch his attention. Everett's heart thumped quickly as he took in loud breaths through his nose.

"What's wrong?" Rhys mumbled with a yawn. "Did you have a nightmare or something?"

"Do you smell that?"

Rhys also took in a deep breath. All he smelled was the remnants of their dinner and the smoke from the fireplace. "What?"

Everett shook his head firmly. "The snow, Rhys, the snow. It's...it's so strong. How can you not smell that? Don't you at least feel the buzzing? Or hear the rumbling?"

At the word "snow," Rhys's eyes widened, all tiredness lost. "Shit, are you saying it's going to snow again?"

He scrambled to stand and rushed over to the window, where he peered through the foggy condensation his breathing created on the cold glass. It was indeed snowing outside, but not too much, only a small sprinkle of snowflakes blowing in the wind—which was oddly quite rough. The gusts of wind created a howling noise and shook loose the snow that clung to the tree branches. But the real, most concerning part were the clouds in the distance, just barely visible as the sun began to rise over the horizon, contrasting the darkness of the clouds to the lightness of the sky they blocked out. If he concentrated hard enough, he could hear the rumbling of the oncoming storm.

"A blizzard. A fucking *blizzard*," Rhys hissed, gripping the wooden windowsill. "You've got to be kidding me! That looks like it might hit within the hour. Shit, what am I going to do? The amount of snow it'll dump on us could block us in for weeks. I guess we're gonna have to use my emergency food and wood supply after all. This is *bad*."

"Will...will that be enough for the both of us?" Everett asked meekly.

Rhys sighed, scrunching his eyes shut and massaging his temples. A migraine was already coming on from the stress. "I don't know. I think if we ration it well, we could last for a month. Which could be enough, as long as the blizzard doesn't stay too long. They usually don't last longer than a few days. So, if that holds true, we could be fine."

"You don't sound so sure about that..." Everett looked down at his feet. "Maybe...maybe it would be best if I left, so I wouldn't use up all of your food—"

"Everett, *no*," Rhys interrupted sternly. "Where would you go if you left, huh?"

Everett was silent for a moment. "Um..."

Rhys sighed again and reached out to hold Everett by his shoulders. Everett peered up at him with his bottom lip bit harshly between his teeth, which looked quite painful. Rhys lifted his thumb up to Everett's mouth and gently tugged the lip free. It was tinged slightly red from a drop of blood, the same color as Everett's cheeks. His eyes were wide, innocent, and terrified, like a deer staring down the barrel of a gun. Even though Rhys was smaller than Everett, a burning desire to protect this adorable creature simmered inside him. How could Everett even think of doing something so dangerous?

"Yeah, that's what I thought. You have nowhere to go," Rhys said, stroking his cheek. "If you left, you'd just freeze and starve to death out there. Don't even think about doing some superhero sacrificial shit so I could survive. I'd rather starve in here together than live because you died in that damn storm. Got it?"

"B-but..." Everett leaned into Rhys's touch in a way that was so incredibly endearing. "I feel really bad about taking all of your resources..."

"No 'but's,' Everett. You're staying here. There's no need to leave, okay? We...we'll be fine. It'll be hard, but we'll make it out of this blizzard alive. Together," Rhys said softly, a smile growing on his face, which Everett returned hesitantly.

"To-together. Yeah."

★

With the snow impeding any efforts to leave the cabin, Rhys and Everett were effectively housebound, and the days began to tick much slower.

For Rhys, it was nothing new. Sure, he greatly missed being able to go outside, but he was perfectly content with spending his days by the fireplace reading a book aloud or completing chores around the cabin. However, for Everett, it was as if he were stuck in a living hell.

The first two days went relatively well, with Everett occupied by assisting Rhys with tasks such as scooping up snow to melt for water storage, patching a small roof leak, and planning out how to ration what food was left in the cellar, as well as napping together. But, as the days continued to pass, Rhys noticed Everett was quickly becoming bored and stir-crazy. At almost any moment, he caught him staring longingly out of the window at the roaring blizzard, whining under his breath. He'd pace around aimlessly when Rhys was occupied with something unrelated to him.

And on the fourth day, Everett's behavior escalated even further. When Everett left for his afternoon outhouse trip, instead of coming back within ten minutes as normal, he didn't return. Nor did he when another ten minutes had passed, worrying Rhys that something bad had happened to him. He quickly shoved on his cleated boots and bundled himself up in his coat. He stepped outside and headed toward the outhouse. Cupping his hands over his mouth, he called out Everett's name over and over again as his heart and his mind raced with the terrifying possibilities.

Maybe Everett had decided to leave after all to make sure Rhys would be able to survive— No, he had agreed he wouldn't do that. He had to have gotten lost. Even though the path between the outhouse and cabin was short, the blizzard was thick enough to blind a person walking through it, and they could accidentally go a bit too far north, passing the cabin. Or he could've injured himself somehow. Even though his leg was closer to being fully healed, if he had taken another nasty fall, it was possible the scab could've reopened. He could've been dragged off by some hungry predator, hit by an object blowing in the wind, fallen into the river, or—

"*Everett!*"

He suddenly appeared out of nowhere into Rhys's field of vision. Not from the outhouse, not from the cabin—instead, from the forest. His teeth were chattering and his lips were blue, but they lifted into a wide grin.

"Everett, what the fuck? What happened to you?" Rhys exclaimed as he pulled the shivering man into a hug. "Did you get lost or something?"

Everett shook his head and wrapped his arms around Rhys as well, hooking his chin over his shoulder. As he talked, his deep voice vibrated against Rhys's neck. "N-no, I wasn't lost... I was just, um, taking a w-walk—"

"Taking a walk? In a blizzard? What were you thinking?" Rhys squawked, pulling back to look up at Everett with a sharp glare. "Fuck, you scared the absolute shit out of me for a *walk*? Why would you do that?"

"I-I'm sorry, okay? I just needed to get out of the cabin for a while!" Everett said, averting his gaze sheepishly. "I didn't mean to worry you... I was only going to be gone for a couple of minutes. I feel a lot better now though!"

"You think I wouldn't be worried when you went missing for twenty minutes? You—*ugh*, it's fucking freezing out here," Rhys grumbled when a particularly brutal gust of icy wind smacked them, almost making them topple over. "Let's talk about this inside."

Pulling Everett behind him, Rhys marched back to the safety of the warm cabin. Rhys sat Everett down in front of the fireplace and cocooned him in a blanket. Then he practically force-fed some hot broth down Everett's throat until his skin tone turned back to normal and his shivering stopped. The entire time, Everett didn't meet Rhys's concerned gaze, instead, he stared into the flames.

"I'm sorry," he whispered, hanging his head low. "I really didn't mean to scare you."

"Look," Rhys said. "I know it's hard being cooped up in here. I *know*. But you really can't be waltzing out into a blizzard. You could have died, Everett. Could've gotten lost on that walk. You've got a good nose, sure. But I doubt you'd be able to sniff your way back to the cabin in a blizzard. So, no matter how bored you are, no matter how much pent-up energy you have, you can never, ever do that again, all right?"

Everett sighed and nodded. "Okay...I understand. I won't do that again."

Rhys chuckled, ruffling his hair, which was still speckled with snowflakes and tangled from the wind. He carefully carded his fingers through it like a comb, gently detangling the strands as Everett peeked up at him.

"You better not! I swear, you almost gave me a heart attack. Thank fuck you're okay though. You and your damn energy. You really need another way to get it out, *safely*. Hmm...*oh*!" Rhys snapped his fingers with a grin, a lightbulb going off inside of his brain. "How about we start your reading and writing lessons, if you'd be up for it?"

"I dunno," Everett said with a shrug. "I don't think I'd be any good at it."

"Nonsense. That's what you thought about hunting, but you did amazing at that too. Trust me, you're plenty smart. I think it could be really good for you in a lot of ways. It's something you need to know to survive and also give you a mental workout. Learning can even be fun, once you can read books yourself. Wouldn't that be nice?"

Everett's lips upturned into a small smile. "That would be nice, actually. I'd love to read to you like you've been doing for me sometime, if that's possible."

An image appeared in Rhys's mind, one that had his cheeks tinging pink, of him and Everett cuddling by the fire, Rhys lying on his rumbling chest as he listened to his deep voice for hours. It certainly would be nice for a change, but also dangerous at the same time. Rhys would have to make sure to keep Everett away from his more risqué books, such as some of the romances that had pretty graphic sex scenes. If Rhys were to listen to Everett describing one of those...he would be a goner for sure.

"I'd like that too," Rhys said, trying to keep his voice as normal-sounding as possible. "I probably have some books that'd be easy to read for a beginner. *Harry Potter*, some poetry books—stuff like that. If we work hard, I'm sure you could even do so within a few weeks or so."

"Really? That fast?"

"Yeah! Like I said, you're smart, Everett. I believe in you."

Everett's face broke into a wide, toothy smile that turned his eyes into little crescents, a face so breathtaking Rhys worried that, maybe, he was already gone for this man.

Fuck.

Chapter Seven

Once again, Rhys had become Everett's teacher. They started off small the next day with the alphabet, after Rhys had spent the evening creating flashcards and worksheets while Everett slept. As expected, Everett was hesitant to learn—the complete opposite of his hunting lessons; most likely, he was still embarrassed at not knowing these basic skills at his age. Rhys tried his best to be patient with him, smiling encouragingly when Everett's hand shook as he awkwardly gripped the pencil. His letters were lopsided and crudely drawn, barely resembling what they were supposed to be.

But as the first and second weeks came and went, Everett once again proved himself to be a star pupil, his confidence growing each day. By the end of the second week, he was able to spell and read simple sentences, sometimes even able to understand more complex words when sounding them out. It was mentally taxing for him, though, so Rhys came up with the idea one day of playing board games as a break.

"So, I have Uno, Sorry, Exploding Kittens, Monopoly—"

"What's a Mon...Mon...Polly?" Everett asked, his eyebrows scrunching in confusion as he attempted to read the names on the boxes.

"Monopoly, Everett, see? You missed the second O," Rhys explained patiently, pointing at each letter. "Anyway, it's the bane of a capitalistic society's existence, pretty much. Well, one of them, at least."

Everett blinked. "Right... Well, the little dude on the box looks weird, so I wanna play it."

"Yeah, okay. Lemme explain the rules." Rhys opened the box and gestured toward the small metal pieces hiding beneath the map. "These little statues are our characters. We pick one, and that statue represents you on the game boa—"

"Ooh, I'll be the wolf," Everett exclaimed, grabbing the dog and holding it to his chest.

"That's a dog— Wait, I thought you were afraid of wolves?"

"W-well, yeah, but *this* wolf isn't real, and it's cute, so I want to be this one," Everett singsonged and stuck his tongue out. "And you should be... Oh! Heh, you should be the boot. It's fitting because you're always stomping on my happiness."

Rhys snorted and rolled his eyes. He should've been annoyed, but the grin on Everett's face just wouldn't let him be anything but fond.

"I don't know about that," he said, "but whatever. I'll be the damn boot. Anyway, these will be our characters that we move around on the board, and this is your money." He handed Everett a stack of fake, colorful bills.

"What...are these?" Everett asked, flipping through them with wide eyes.

"Don't tell me you've never even heard of *money* before," Rhys said in a deadpan tone with a shake of his head. "I swear to god, your family... *Anyway*, it's money. Each color has a different value which can be traded for things. When you land on a property, you have the option to buy it with a certain amount of money. If someone has already bought it before you, then you have to pay them rent. The goal is to collect as many properties as possible so you can bleed the other player dry."

"Money," Everett whispered in fascination. "Interesting. But if I want your property, why can't I just take it from you in a fight?"

"Because this isn't a war. That's called *stealing*, Everett, and stealing is bad."

Everett nodded slowly. "Okay...stealing *bad*, money *good*. I think I get it, so can we play already?"

It was supposed to be a piece of cake for Rhys to win the game, playing against someone who hadn't even seen a single board game in his life. After often playing Monopoly online with strangers during his childhood, Rhys had learned the perfect strategy to win. Screw Park Place and Boardwalk—supposedly the most coveted properties—the real way to win was to buy up all of the reds, oranges, and railroads. Landing on the dark blue properties would completely ruin a player's chance at winning, but it was incredibly unlikely that would happen multiple times. Slow and steady would win the race.

Everett, having no idea which properties were more valuable than others, was naïve to Rhys's plan. When he was offered large sums of money, or a few of the useless properties, so Rhys could buy his desired ones, Everett would happily take the trade with a shit-eating grin, as if Rhys were the sucker. Rhys almost felt bad for taking advantage of him. *Almost*. It was a competition after all, one he wanted to win as per usual. And at this rate, he was definitely going to do so, now that he'd gotten the three sets, which he would soon load up with hotels.

Or so Rhys had thought. Up until he landed on Everett's Boardwalk, and its hotel charged him a whopping two grand—more cash than he had on hand. There was no way he'd be able to win, leaving Everett giggling like a gleeful maniac, extremely pleased with himself.

"You *bastard*!" Rhys squawked. "How did your strategy even work? You shouldn't have been able to win playing like that! Boardwalk and Park Place never work, and you spent all of your money on them!"

"Oh, don't be such a sore loser, Rhys." Everett reached over to boop Rhys's nose. "Maybe you can win the next round."

Rhys huffed as he packed up the board back into its box. "You want us to play again? No fucking way. I don't play with *cheaters*."

"And how am *I* a cheater? You were the one sticking his little thieving hands into the bank when I got up to get you a cup of water! I thought you said stealing was *bad*."

"That never happened. You have no proof," Rhys exclaimed, pointing an accusatory finger. "You...you...*ugh*. I don't know how you cheated, but you must have!"

"Well, honestly, at first I didn't really know what I was doing, but I think I caught on pretty fast." Everett snickered with an evil grin. "But I never cheated. I'm just that good, and you're just that bad."

"You know what? I think I am actually up for round two. I'm gonna make you regret saying that!"

Though the first round of Monopoly had lasted only a couple of hours, the second one was worse. The battle between the two stubborn men raged on for multiple days, both so wrapped up in their vendettas to care about any of their basic needs, not even sleep nor meals. Eventually, though, the lack of self-care took a toll on their bodies, leaving them passed out across the board from exhaustion on day four, with indents in their cheeks in the shape of the little plastic hotels.

At first, when they awoke twelve hours later, they were reasonably upset that they had completely messed up the setup on the board, making it impossible to pick their game back up again from where they'd left off. However, neither of them could find it in themselves to care about their unresolved war when their stomachs growled and begged for food so loudly.

After three whole days of starving themselves for the sake of Monopoly, Rhys made the executive decision to divvy up the rabbit stew at twice the rationed amount. They wolfed it down like starved, ravenous animals, barely pausing in between their heaping spoonfuls to breathe.

Once their stomachs were happy and the dishes were cleaned, they shoved the abandoned Monopoly board to the side so they could settle down comfortably in front of the fireplace, sitting close as they took sips of chamomile tea. Their shoulders pressed together only added to the pleasant warmth from their meal that had brought a healthy tinge of pink to both of their cheeks.

"You know, you really impressed me today—or should I say, over the last three days," Rhys commented after a long stretch of silence, and he turned to look at Everett with a small smile.

"Huh? What did I do?" Everett asked, cocking his head to the side.

"Oh, no need to act all shy about it." Rhys chuckled fondly. "For someone who has never played a board game and has only just recently begun learning how to read, you play one *hell* of a game. Gave me a real run for my money."

Rhys's smile only grew as he watched Everett's pink cheeks suddenly burst into scarlet-red.

"N-Nah, it was nothing, really," Everett sputtered as he rubbed at the back of his neck, avoiding Rhys's gaze in favor of looking down into his empty mug.

"Nothing, huh? You call beating me twice in a row *nothing*?" Rhys snorted, playfully shoving Everett's shoulder. "You got some nerve. Just take the compliment, okay? You did great. Really good. Top-tier Monopoly player. I bet you could even take on the Monopoly champion world record holder for most wins. I bet—"

"*Stop it!*" Everett squeaked, reaching out to slap a hand over Rhys's mouth. "You're saying things! Weird things!"

"No, I'm completely serious," Rhys insisted. "You're my student, so let me compliment you, let me be proud of you!"

"You're so embarrassing," Everett grumbled as he hid his burning face behind his knees. "You're even worse than my siblings."

If Rhys's ears had been able to perk up like a dog's, they would've at those words. For the entire time Everett had been living with him, it had been rare for him to mention anything about his family, which left Rhys hungry for more details, yet careful of overstepping his bounds.

"Yeah? Did they tease you too?" Rhys asked.

Everett nodded. "All of the time. Too much, really. I guess that's what I get for being the youngest."

Though Rhys wasn't all that experienced with the plight of having siblings, he thought he could understand. As a young child, he'd played often enough with the family of five sisters next door to see the elders excluding the youngest from playing their Princesses-and-the-Prince dress-up game. He'd always made sure to ask his mother every day for an extra cookie in his lunch box to give to her to make up for it.

"How many siblings do you have?"

"Um." Everett peeked up to count on his fingers with furrowed brows. "Uh, twenty-eight, I think? Sixteen brothers and twelve sisters. Though, if I count the ones who didn't make it—"

"Wait, wait, *twenty-eight*?" Rhys interrupted with a squawk. "How is that even possible? I've never heard of a family that big before, not even the fucking Duggars have that many kids! Oh my god, please don't tell me they all have names starting with *E* or some shit."

There was a long stretch of silence before Everett answered, finally sitting up, face now clear of the blush. "Is that not...normal?" he asked slowly. "The other...er...family near us had forty!"

Jesus Christ, Rhys thought. Rest in peace to those poor women and their vaginas. The more Everett revealed about his family and his past, the more Rhys was convinced he'd escaped from some sort of cult. To have that many children by one woman seemed physically impossible—there must have been multiple women pumping out babies from the same father or something. But Rhys didn't voice his suspicions.

"Well, usually," he said instead, "most families only have two or three. Damn, it must be hard for your parents to feed everyone, huh?"

Everett nodded again. "*Really* hard. I was always the smallest, so I couldn't push past the others all that well to get to the food."

"No way! *You're* the smallest?" Rhys scanned Everett up and down, from his thick fingers to his long, *long* legs. "There's nothing small about you, you're *huge*! A fucking giant compared to my short ass! Oh god, your family must be, like, seven feet tall if you're the smallest."

"Well, *now* I'm bigger 'cuz I got older, but when I was a kid, I was tiny. Maybe even tinier than you." Everett snickered, which earned him a swat from Rhys.

"Cheeky brat," Rhys grumbled with a playful glare. "Now, how about you put your giant self to good use and be my space heater, hmm? I'm ready to knock the fuck out right now."

Everett's lips stretched into a wide grin. "Gladly."

Chapter Eight

Rhys was numb to the pain when he dug his jagged fingernails into his palms so hard they almost broke through the calloused skin. In fact, he couldn't feel much of anything these days, not with the permanent chill in his bones. There was no escaping the cold, no matter how ferocious the fire roared in its futile attempts to defend them from it. It seeped in through the cracks in the mortar that held the log walls together. Through the snow piling up on the roof that was bound to cave in any day now. Through the uninsulated doorframe. Through the thin single-pane windows frosted over with ice—even if he were to somehow chip it off, he still wouldn't have been able to see a single thing, only white.

It had been an entire month since the blizzards first started, and there seemed to be no end to their wrath in sight. Rhys was well aware of how rough winters up here in the mountains could be, with two of them under his belt, yet this one was different, as if Mother Nature really did have it in for the two of them.

He had always commended himself for his perfect planning skills, but there was no way he could prepare for what he couldn't foresee.

The storms did take breathers every few days or so, but when they did, it seemed to be only for a few hours while they slept—as if mocking Rhys, teasing him for what he couldn't have, dangling it out of his desperate reach. The food stockpile couldn't last forever, after all. Even if they were to ration servings minuscule enough to keep them alive, there still wouldn't be close to enough to last them until the day spring found them, giving them reprieve.

Maybe, if Everett weren't there, Rhys might've been able to just squeeze by with his life hanging by a thread, though that wasn't a thought he wanted to entertain for even a second.

To pass the time, Rhys had tried his best to distract Everett from the inevitable threat of their untimely demise and the incessant rumbling of their empty stomachs. There wasn't much use in Everett learning how to read and write now with no foreseeable future in which he could put his new skills to good use, though he stayed Rhys's diligent student. Now, as he wrote out sentences describing himself and Rhys, his hand shook from the cold, no longer from a lack of confidence.

Rhys had attempted to distract himself as well by putting all of his energy into his teaching and filling every other moment ravenously reading through his expansive book collection. But just as there was no physical escape from the cold, he couldn't break free mentally either. The fear of dying followed him into his sleep, causing brutal nightmares that had him thrashing and screaming, only calmed by Everett waking him up and holding him close to his chest, whispering soothing words. He'd thankfully never asked what they were about. If Rhys were to tell him he dreamt of finding Everett dead and cold next to him, his skin tinged blue, he thought he might vomit up all of the precious, tiny meals he needed to keep down.

But now, as Rhys stared into the expanse of the almost empty cellar, nails threatening to leave angry crescent-shaped scars in his palms, it was clear he could no longer ignore the screaming, panicking voice in the back of his head. There was no way either Rhys or Everett would die without putting up one last fight, one last attempt at ensuring survival. With only a week's worth of emergency food left, Rhys finally decided to take the risk.

"No, Rhys, you can't," Everett pleaded, tugging Rhys back by his wrist, his eyes glassy with unshed, desperate tears. "It's too dangerous."

"I have to, Everett." Rhys yanked his hand back and turned toward the door. "There's no other choice. I have to do this."

Before he could reach out to turn the knob, Everett rushed over to slam his back against the door, blocking Rhys's exit. "Then at least let me come with you."

"I've already said *no*. You aren't coming with me."

"And why the hell not? Rhys, you can't go ice fishing in the middle of the fucking night, *alone*! Why would you think that's a good idea? Didn't you say yourself that being alone out there is dangerous? You're just asking for some hungry bear or wolf or something to come eat you! Or what if the storm starts up again before you can get back and you can't find your way home and freeze to death out there and I can never find your body and—"

"*Everett*," Rhys barked at him. Everett, who had begun to breathe harshly, shut his mouth at the commanding tone. Rhys extended his hand to cradle Everett's cheek. "I'm going to be fine. It's different from when you went out. I'm actually prepared."

"B-but—"

"First of all, the blizzard is calm right now. And second of all, the bears are hibernating right now, farther down in the valley with the wolves and such. No predator is going to bother to come up to this elevation for food, no matter how hungry. There's no good prey up here. They know better than that," Rhys explained slowly. "And I'm not going far, no more than a quarter of a mile. I'll be able to find my way back. Unlike when you went out, I'll leave markers on the path I take, just to be safe, and carry a compass. You have nothing to be worried about. If you need something to worry about, then just pray I'll come back with a whole bag full of fish."

The first tear rolled down Everett's face, which Rhys was quick to wipe away with his gloved thumb.

"But st-still, can't I come with you?" Everett sobbed. "E-even if what you say is true, I can at least be another set of hands to fish. We can get m-more if I'm there."

"You don't even know how to fish, silly." Rhys curled his lips into a fond smile, touched by Everett's insistence. But nothing could change his mind. No way would he risk Everett's life in addition to his own. "You'd be a lot more help staying here and tending the fire while I'm gone. Don't want me to come back to a freezing cold house, now do you?"

Everett sniffled. "No," he whispered with a small shake of his head.

"Then take good care of the fire for me, all right? And I'll be back before you know it."

★

The trek down to the river was just as treacherous as Rhys had expected it to be. It wasn't all that far from the cabin, but with the snow piled up almost as tall as Rhys, it took a tremendous amount of effort to trudge through it with his faithful snowshoes, leaving him out of breath and weak by the time he finally reached his destination. The river was completely frozen over with a thick layer of ice that would've withstood the weight of a car, so it was perfectly safe for Rhys to walk across without fear of it breaking and drowning him. He chose a spot above the deepest section, where he set up a folding chair and cut a large hole in the ice with his saw. He baited his three lines with maggots from his compost pile and dropped them into the water.

Thankfully, the blizzard had calmed relatively, though it was still just as cold. The wind made Rhys shiver violently, combined with the dark sky. He stared up toward the endless expanse of stars, eyes following each constellation easily with muscle memory.

There'd been times when Rhys had considered giving up this life, forcing him to think about moving back to civilization to battle his mental illnesses. But there was just something about the night sky out here that reeled him back every single time. In the city, with all of its bright, unnatural lights, there wasn't much to see. Here, he could see everything, as if he could reach out and swirl up the galaxies with his index finger, like stirring the contents of his soup bowl. His troubles seemed nonexistent and trivial when he was reminded of just how small he was in comparison to space itself. He was just another lump of stardust floating aimlessly.

To others, the thought might've been frightening or saddening, but to Rhys, it was the opposite—there was no need to worry nor to stress when the weight of the world rested in the balance of space rather than on his own shoulders.

Hours ticked by until the sun began to rise over the horizon, bathing Rhys with a slight tingling warmth and light that brought him back down to Earth, back into the fight for survival. In the distance, storm clouds rolled closer, so he knew it was time to go back home, lest he confirm Everett's fears and get lost out here.

When he arrived, it was to Everett throwing open the door and running out into the snow with nothing but his pajamas on. He hugged Rhys so tightly he knocked the breath out of him.

"You're back! Oh my god, I was so worried!" Everett exclaimed, his smile so bright it rivaled the rising sun. "Did you catch anything?"

"Yeah, I did, actually," Rhys said as they walked back into the warm cabin, fire perfectly tended. He shrugged off his winter clothing before opening up his backpack to reveal his bounty.

Everett gasped. "Whoa, Rhys— There's so many of them! Like...*hundreds* of them!"

Rhys chuckled. "Nah, more like twenty or so, and they're not all that big, but it's still a pretty good haul. Might even last us a month if we pace ourselves right. Here, how about I cook one up for us right now, yeah? We can even break out some of the special seasonings to celebrate."

Everett seemed unable to contain his excitement, nearly tripping as he ran over to the kitchen to pull out the little baggie of dried herbs. Together, they gutted, deboned, seasoned, and grilled the fish, filling the cabin with a savory scent that had both of them drooling. It had been a long time only eating rabbit stew, so fish was a welcome change to their bland diet. As always, they scarfed down their dinners—barely making time to savor the taste—before lounging in front of the fire with happy stomachs.

"I was so worried about you," Everett said as he cuddled into Rhys's side. "I don't think I blinked even once staring out the window watching for you."

"You looked out the window for me the entire time?" Rhys laughed, ruffling Everett's hair. "What dedication. Now you know how I felt when you ran out into the storm."

Everett didn't hesitate to lean into Rhys's touch. "That was one time. And I've already apologized for it. I know that wasn't smart of me, and I'll never do it again."

Rhys hummed but didn't answer in words, much too tired from staying up the entire night fishing and already blinking back sleep from heavy eyelids. When his hand went limp atop Everett's head, it was his turn to card through Rhys's hair. But Rhys didn't mind one single bit, falling asleep peacefully in his arms.

★

The next time Rhys awoke, instead of being cold, he was warm—more like *burning hot*, scorching to the touch like the fireplace was roaring inside his very body. Combined with the wicked throbbing in his head, he felt like absolute garbage lit on fire.

Everett was leaning over the fireplace ladling something from the kettle into a mug and whirled around at Rhys's low groan. He set down the mug and rushed over to Rhys's side to help him sit up with a steady hand on his back.

"Finally, you're awake! How are you feeling, Rhys?"

"Not good," Rhys slurred. He sighed at the pleasant coolness of Everett's palm pushing his greasy fringe out of his eyes.

Worry was evident on Everett's face in the form of furrowed eyebrows and a deep-set frown. "Yup, you're still very warm. At least you're awake now though. I was really worried. Still am, to be honest. But I think I have something that can help you feel a bit better."

Everett stood back up, grabbed the mug, and headed over to the kitchen. He rustled through the cabinets for a moment, mumbling something under his breath before he pulled out the jar of honey and scooped a spoonful into the mug.

"How…long was I out?" Rhys asked.

"A day or so. Thought you were just really tired, but then I felt how warm you were, and I knew you were getting really sick— Here, take a sip of this."

Rhys complied, again letting Everett hold him up as he tipped the mug against his lips. His senses were overwhelmed by the taste, warmth, and scent of chamomile tea mixed with a generous amount of honey that coated and soothed his scratchy throat. Though the tea was a bit too hot, it was a welcome sensation after feeling so incredibly parched, as if he had eaten handfuls of sand.

"Is it good? I wasn't sure if I made it right," Everett said quietly, biting his bottom lip.

"'S good. *Really* good." Rhys smiled weakly. "Thank you, Everett."

"Nah, nah, no need to thank me, silly!" Everett waved one hand dismissively while the other scratched at his nape. The motion dragged Rhys's attention over to the table behind Everett, its wooden surface strewn with that seemed to be Rhys's entire collection of cups and mugs. Rhys assumed they were most likely taste tests of failed batches of tea—he had to hold back a fond giggle at the sight.

"Enough about me though," Everett continued. "I know you feel like shit right now, but is there anything I can get or do for you at all? Another pillow? Blanket? Food? You must be *starving*! I tried to force you to drink some broth, but I think I mostly just dumped it all onto you by accident."

At that, Rhys actually let out a laugh that had him coughing in only a matter of seconds.

"N-no wonder I smell like fish," he managed to say through the fit.

"Don't make fun of me. I'm trying my best. It's the thought that counts, right?" Everett whined, pulling his signature pout.

"Yes, it was a sweet gesture. Thank you." Rhys pinched Everett's pink, embarrassed cheeks. "Anyway, I actually *am* quite hungry. I wouldn't mind a bit of soup right now."

Everett nodded, taking Rhys's mug and refilling it with more tea before he turned his attention to the pot simmering next to the kettle. When he removed the cast iron lid, the cabin was flooded with the familiar scent of the fish Rhys had caught, causing his mouth to water despite the dryness of his throat. Carefully, Everett ladled scoop after scoop into a bowl, seemingly taking extra care to grab as many chunks of meat that he could.

"Hey, uh, Everett," Rhys spoke up, brows furrowed. Everett turned to him with a hum and a cocked head. "Isn't that way too big of a portion you're making for me? Like, almost triple the rationed amount?"

Everett's cheeks colored pink again. "Uh, yeah..."

He cleared his throat and averted his gaze, looking down at the heaping serving of soup as if surprised he had filled the bowl that much. "Yeah, I've kind of been...not eating while you were out."

"And *why* the fuck would you do that?"

"Been much too worried to eat, I guess," Everett said with a sheepish shrug. "I tried, but worrying makes me nauseous. Besides, I thought I should save my portions for you. You're sick. You need to eat as much as you can to get better. I can go a few days without."

Rhys wanted to be, and should've been, upset at Everett for denying himself his deserved meals—for Rhys's sake of all things—but with him looking as if he might cry if scolded, Rhys didn't have the heart to do so over something so kind and selfless. For *him* of all people.

"Well, thank you, but at least give yourself a little something to eat, okay? Even if you're not hungry. You can't help me get better if you're dying from malnutrition yourself."

"Hmph. Fine, but let me feed you first." Everett shuffled over on his knees across the furs to hold out a heaping spoonful to Rhys. "Okay, here you go! Open up now; I promise I won't spill it on you this time!"

As he fed Rhys, Everett made sure to keep a hand under the spoon so as to not let it drip. The soup was just as soothing to the sickness brewing in Rhys as the tea was, if not more. With his nose so congested, he couldn't enjoy the rich taste as much as he normally would've, much to his annoyance. When he did finally persuade Everett that he'd had his fill after swallowing down over half of the obscenely large portion, Everett did keep his other promise as well, finishing off what was left in the bowl—with the *same spoon*.

Rhys wasn't sure whether he should've felt utterly revolted or flustered as all hell at the sight. Everett licked the soup residue off of the spoon like it was a lollipop, his long tongue curling around it, dipping in to lap against the curvature, even letting out a small, pleased moan at the savory taste. Yup, flustered, Rhys was definitely flustered. His entire face burned a deep scarlet, hotter than his fever. How could he *not* be flustered, when that spoon had just been in his own mouth? In a way, it was pretty much an indirect kiss, one Everett appeared to be enjoying. For a split second, Rhys wished the spoon was him.

He panicked for a moment, remembering how he hadn't brushed his teeth for at least two days, so there was no way Everett should've been remotely enjoying this. And what the fuck, neither should've *Rhys* because there was absolutely nothing attractive about this situation at all, not in the slightest. What was *wrong* with him? It had to be his fever turning him delirious or something.

And there was no time to think on that either, since Rhys should've been way more worried about Everett catching his sickness from swapping spit with him. Had he never learned about contagious viruses before? Who shared food with a sick person?

"Everett, no! Go get your own. You're gonna get your dumb ass sick as well if you do that," Rhys squawked in renewed disgust and panic, lunging forward to snatch the utensil. But Everett leaned back away from him too quickly.

"But that means even more dishes that I don't wanna wash," Everett protested, holding the spoon out as far away from Rhys as he could reach. "Besides, you don't have to worry about me getting sick. I never get sick."

Rhys couldn't keep up his disbelieving glare when he was forced to cough violently again.

"Bullshit," he said once it calmed down. "Everyone gets sick at least once in their lives. What, are you telling me you have a magically strong immune system too?"

"Mm-hmm. Never gotten sick, not even when I was young." Everett beamed proudly when he stuck the spoon back into his mouth, the utensil bobbing up and down as he spoke, clinking against his teeth. "Well, now that I think about it, I have had an upset stomach a few times, like, from eating things I wasn't supposed to, but not like you have. And I was weak for a winter when we didn't have enough food. What did you call it again, by the way? The sickness you have? My family just called it winter sickness."

Rhys wasn't too convinced, though he was much too tired and loopy to argue that Everett probably had been sick before but just didn't remember it.

"The flu," he answered with a yawn. "It's actually been a while since I've had it, even though I haven't been vaccinated since I moved out here—and no, before you ask, I'm not like those weird-ass antivax suburban white moms named Karen who think vaccines cause autism. I just don't have the time or energy to make an appointment and drive all of the way down there."

Everett blinked rapidly. "Wait, wait, wait, slow down. Uh, what's a vaccine? Antivax? And who the fuck is *Karen*?"

For a moment, the room was silent, and then Rhys broke into a flurry of laughter at the sight of poor Everett's utterly confused face. It wasn't so much laughter as coughing once again, so hard that Everett put aside being annoyed at being left out of the joke to help Rhys sit up to clear his cough more effectively. His entire body shook, and his throat burned for what felt like hours of mind-numbing, awful pain—he really regretted not getting his vaccinations now. Clearly, even hundreds of miles away from proper civilization, he could still somehow catch the dreaded flu.

"Maybe you should be going to sleep again," Everett said, brows furrowed in concern as he patted Rhys's back and supported him in drinking another warm cup of honeyed tea.

Rhys nodded weakly, unable to speak, trying his best to make his appreciation known with a smile as Everett gently tucked him back into the piles of blankets. He then blew out all of the candles, leaving the fire hot and lit—though Rhys felt much warmer when Everett settled down next to him and wrapped his arms tightly around him, holding him close.

Chapter Nine

Naturally, like any other person, Rhys had never enjoyed being sick. Back when he lived in the big city, it felt as if he was sick all day every day, whether from his allergies to dust and smoke that would make his eyes water and nose run or from catching yet another cold from touching the snot-slicked handles on the bus. Medicine had become his best friend—he bought so much of the stuff he swore the old lady who ran his local pharmacy was beginning to think he was running an underground drug ring.

Even as a young child, he was forced to fend for himself during his constant bouts of illness, with his parents working too many long hours to be able to stay home to care for him, when he'd spend weeks on end coughing his lungs out like some sort of child smoker.

And unfortunately, when Rhys was older, it hadn't been much better. His two short-term boyfriends hadn't seen taking care of him as important enough to call out of their own jobs or even come over to check on him after their shifts. Neither had his handful of friends. To be fair, Rhys never explicitly asked anyone to help him out, but he'd thought taking care of one another was something family, friends, and partners should be happy to do without being asked—which turned out, time and time again, to have been another one of Rhys's unreachable dreams.

It sucked majorly, though he'd gotten used to taking care of himself, even coming to enjoy it in a weird way, as he'd never been one to be a burden to others. He could handle himself just fine, thank you very much. He didn't need anybody.

Yet, no matter how many times he insisted he could do so, Everett wouldn't take no for an answer, persisting in doing everything and anything he could to assist Rhys. Over the next week, as the flu held his body captive, it was as if their roles had completely switched, with Everett now the caretaker and Rhys the one in need.

As the days ticked by with no sign of Everett backing down, Rhys eventually realized that, deep down, *maybe*, he secretly reveled in being cared for so attentively for the first time in his life. Never would he ever admit it aloud, but there was no way in hell he could've found it in himself to be upset at Everett's genuine expressions of kindness. Rhys couldn't be, not when Everett looked so happy in everything he did, like cooking all of their meals.

But there were still many instances where Rhys desperately wished he didn't need the help. The sickness was so harrowing that he was unable to hobble to the outhouse by himself without losing his balance from the dizziness, forcing him to be carried to and from instead, which was so incredibly embarrassing.

It was even worse when Rhys found himself unable to wash his body. He tried valiantly at first, but quickly realized there was no way his weak noodle-arms could repeatedly lift and tip the buckets full of warm water to rinse the soap off, as well as scrub his skin with the loofa. He was forced to call in Everett, who'd been waiting right outside the door to the bathing room, to do those things for him. It was nothing short of extremely humiliating having been unable to do such a simple task, especially since he had to be naked in front of Everett.

"D-don't look," Rhys mumbled.

As Everett stood in the doorway, still as a statue with his jaw clenched, Rhys shrank in on himself, feeling very small and vulnerable in the big tub and under Everett's heavy gaze. There was nowhere to hide his body. He must've looked a strange sight with his wavy hair now straight and flattened against his head and his body all sudsed up, shivering and cowering like a terrified Chihuahua.

The air was tense and silent for a moment before Everett seemingly came to his senses, snapping out of his reverie to blush scarlet and slap his palms over his eyes.

"I-I'm so sorry, oh my god." Everett exclaimed, shaking his head. "I really didn't mean to—*shit*—um, are you sure you want me to do this? I really don't want to make you uncomfortable—"

"Just shut up, don't look, and dump that water on me, okay? I'm freezing in here, and I just want to get this over with already. The water's gonna get cold."

"R-right, got it..."

Looking anywhere but at Rhys, Everett grabbed one of the buckets filled with now lukewarm water and slowly let it cascade upon Rhys's head. As it trickled down to pool at the bottom of the tub, Rhys was mortified that he was beginning to get hard. Quickly, before Everett could notice, he covered his nether regions with his hands. He couldn't believe his annoying body. Only seconds ago, he was completely soft from the cold and embarrassment, and now that there was a man—an attractive man—looming over him, his dick decided to get riled up.

What was wrong with him? Had the last few tiny shreds of his dignity just gotten washed away with the soap? There was nothing arousing about this scenario in the slightest, yet again! He thought he'd gotten some control over his attraction to Everett during the last week, but it must have been the illness suppressing it. And now that he was feeling slightly better, his traitorous brain decided to make the situation even more awkward.

As he bit his bottom lip harshly and clenched his eyes shut, Rhys tried to imagine anything else to will himself to go soft again and reminded himself about how being attracted and actually wanting to *act* on attraction were completely different things. And later that night, he had to remind himself yet again when a sleeping someone's hand rested on his inner thigh.

But as he was busy spending all his energy remaining faithful to their platonic relationship, he didn't notice he was neglecting something else, something more important, until it was too late. He was in much too deep to escape from being attracted to Everett emotionally, not just physically.

Rhys realized his grave mistake when Everett was engrossed in reading a book out loud for the first time.

It'd been an easy read, one of the few poetry books Rhys had stocked in his library. Despite it being almost a hundred years old, he had read the compilation of poems all of the way through at least twenty times. He was glad he'd decided to impulse buy it years ago at a thrift store because of the beautiful, hand-painted watercolor of the very forest he lived in on the cover. The author was unknown, yet the way they stitched together just a few lines of simple words into images and emotions made Rhys feel as if he'd known the person all of his life, or as if he *were* them, seeing through their eyes.

He had fallen in love with it a while ago, but as Everett read it aloud in that husky, deep tone of his, curled up together next to the fire, Rhys found himself falling in love a second time.

It didn't matter that Everett was still quite new at reading—his stuttering and pauses enhanced the poems in a way Rhys couldn't ever hope to explain in his own words.

"The b-bear steps out into the wintear—win*ter*," Everett narrated, an index finger underlining the words as he read to keep his place. It was the longest of all of the pieces, and Rhys's personal favorite. "Snow rushes to...to...cover its tracks."

While Rhys should've been focusing on how quickly Everett had learned to read in the span of only a month or so, he found himself instead staring at the mole below his lips as they formed each word so carefully, as if caressing them, just as soft as his hands always were with Rhys. Everett's thick brows furrowed when he got stuck on a word, his bottom lip sticking out in a pout. When he turned the page, Rhys's heart skipped a beat at the sight of Everett's smile, dimples making themselves known at the watercolor of a brown bear cloaked in snow. The small grin was contagious, causing Rhys's weak lips to twitch into one as well. He was grateful for the lack of sufficient light in the cabin, or his blush would have been very easily visible.

"...Rhys? Did I pronounce that right?"

The same deep tone that had lulled Rhys into a sense of sleepy longing jerked him back into reality, his smile dropping as quickly as it had appeared.

Everett's was gone, too, replaced with a concerned frown that had Rhys's heart aching for the loss. "Hey, are you okay?" he asked slowly, reaching up to feel Rhys's forehead. "You zoned out a bit there."

"Uh, y-yeah, sorry, I'm just...er...tired?" Rhys mumbled, biting his lip nervously and averting his gaze. He hadn't realized he'd stopped listening to the poem. "Sorry, what were you asking me?"

A soft chuckle filled the room, one that sounded fond. "Were you falling asleep on me? If you're tired, you can just tell me, you know. Should we call it a day and go to bed now, hmm?"

"N-no!" Rhys blurted, voice a little too loud. "No." His croaky voice softened as he waved his hand dismissively. He definitely was tired as all hell, but he would much rather let Everett finish this last poem. "It's okay. I'm okay. Keep going."

Everett quirked an eyebrow, as if to protest, but then he shook his head with another smile and went back to reading quietly. Once again, he easily entrapped Rhys back into the hypnosis of his voice. This time, it was made all the better when Everett pulled him into his lap, letting Rhys's back rest against his chest, bearing his small weight.

Rhys sat there in surprise for a split second before he registered what had just happened with wide eyes. He went to flop off of Everett's lap, but Everett was quick to wrap an arm around his waist, holding him there.

"What the—" Rhys hissed, straining to look up at his face.

"Shhh," Everett purred into his ear, his chin propped on Rhys's shoulder. "This is more comfortable. We can both get a good view of the pictures this way."

Indeed, Rhys could see the pages better from here than where he'd previously been leaning against Everett's side, but now he couldn't focus on the pictures or the words, not when he could *feel* the rumbling vibrations from Everett talking as well as the gentle beat of his heart. They'd spooned plenty of times before, but this was different, more intimate. He wouldn't be able to fight it even if he wanted to, which he decided he really didn't want to at all, not when he felt more at peace here than anywhere else in the entire world. The forest itself couldn't compare, hold him this tightly, speak this sweetly, warm him this well, nor take care of him in the way he'd only dreamed about before.

Couldn't love him this way either.

Love. *Love.* It was love emanating from everything Everett did and was. Surprisingly, the this didn't scare Rhys. He'd never been truly loved before, nor had he loved anyone in return, but there was no denying the connection between them. It felt *right* somehow, just like the first time he'd stepped into the forest. Like he belonged here in Everett's arms, cherished and cared for, something precious and irreplaceable. He wasn't quite sure if he deserved this level of affection. But he knew for certain *Everett* deserved every single ounce of love Rhys could've ever hoped to give him, even if he didn't have much he could possibly offer.

And so, as all the other creatures of Earth had done, Rhys ran on pure, wild instinct—the instinct to reach out toward that which he so strongly desired.

Only love guided Rhys when he interrupted the final words of the poem. Only love guided him when he closed the book and set it to the side. Only love guided him when he turned around in Everett's slackened grip. Only love guided him when he silently pressed a gentle hand against Everett's soft, warm cheek, his thumb mapping the sharp line of his jaw. Only love guided him when he leaned in, closer, closer, and closer still, until he was so close he pressed his face against Everett's chest to feel the stuttered heartbeat in his soul, matching his own.

Only love guided him when he opened his lips, ready to whisper the words—but before he could manage to, a pair of lips pressed atop his head, so gentle that it made his own heart swell almost painfully behind his ribcage.

Love, *fuck*, he was so in love he thought he might die from it before his flu could take him out first. That was a death he wouldn't mind, one where his last breaths would be swallowed by Everett's kiss, where he wouldn't feel the cold sting of death, only the warmth of his love holding him close, where the lullaby that emanated from Everett's heart would lull him into eternal slumber.

That night, he didn't ever say the words that tried so desperately to be let out and heard. But it was okay because the kiss he pressed to Everett's heart in return was enough.

For now.

★

As Rhys's love strengthened, his body only weakened. It was almost as if he'd made a trade, a deal with the devil gone wrong, love for life.

In reality, Rhys knew that that wasn't the case, though he *swore* every time he saw Everett's blinding smile aimed at him, or heard his squeaky laughter filling the cabin with joy, he lost minutes off of his life—like eating a piece of bacon or smoking a cigarette indulgence. Instead, if there had to be someone to blame for his condition, he might've turned to curse Mother Nature to hell.

She seemed to have some sort of grudge against Rhys, despite his attempts over the years at living in the forest and respecting all of the animals and plants he came across. The only thing he thought he could've possibly done wrong was killing the animals to sustain himself, but that couldn't be it, not when the lack of hunting for food was the reason Rhys was caught up in this mess.

He and Everett were starving, plain and simple.

As expected, the fish didn't last them long, only two weeks or so, nor did the blizzards give them a second to safely go ice fishing again. If it was possible, the storm outside seemed as though it had grown even stronger, more violent, the winds swirling with hail so quickly one might've mistaken them for a tornado. They'd run through the last few remaining stacks of firewood as well, forcing them to turn to breaking apart various pieces of wooden furniture and cabinets to feed the waning flames. This they rationed, too, only warming the cabin enough to keep frostbite from eating them alive.

However, there was nothing to stop their own stomach acid from eating away at their intestines. Combined with Rhys's ever-present flu, he'd become a skeleton of his past self, ribs sticking out and once-soft cheeks sinking in on themselves. Everett wasn't much better, but he was still significantly stronger without having the flu—though that wouldn't last much longer.

Rhys absolutely loathed how concerned and downright frightened Everett seemed—hated that he was the cause of such distress. They now spent their days wrapped around each other almost twenty-four seven. Everett only moved to tend to Rhys's needs, such as forcing him to drink—water wasn't filling at all, but it was all they had—holding his limp body up even though his own shook from the effort.

The coughing fits grew longer and louder, causing Rhys to collapse backward onto the furs after the sudden bursts of hacking, usually after drinking. Everett panicked every time, asking over and over again if he was okay, to which Rhys nodded weakly, trying his best to put on a smile for his sake, even though it hurt. His fever returned with a vengeance three days into not eating, leaving him groaning in constant discomfort. He assured Everett he was fine, but it was clear he wasn't buying it a single bit.

They both knew he was going to die, and soon.

During the fifth day of his illness, Rhys barely had any moments of lucidity, in and out of fitful moments of sleep, silent sobs of pain ripping through his chest. He clutched Everett's hand as hard as he could, barely strong enough to even lace their fingers together. Scorching to the touch, yet shivering like mad, and so feverish he was sent into seizures.

He was incredibly terrified of dying and leaving Everett alone without anyone to comfort him in his last moments as he'd done for him. And even now, with Everett's eyes filling with tears and throat raw from his begging screams, Rhys still saw love in his eyes, in the tears that landed on his face, and in his words. Love surrounded him.

Love was a powerful thing, but it could never be enough to stop death. It could never be enough to quell the insurmountable grief of losing a loved one either, though Rhys hoped his final words would at least bring one last smile to Everett's face.

"I love you," he whispered quietly, like how a feather might sound. Everett whipped his head up from where it rested on Rhys's chest, eyes wide in disbelief.

"Wh-what?" Everett said just as softly, leaning in close. "What did you just say?"

Rhys was running out of energy, but he somehow found enough to speak again. "I love you, Everett. L-love you so much; you know that, r-right? Please tell me you do—"

Everett sniffled, tears falling again, though he was smiling, the corners of his lips shaking. "Y-you do?"

Rhys answered with a small nod and a matching smile. Only warmth surrounded him at his love's embrace, so tight yet so gentle.

"Remember me when I'm gone," he murmured into Everett's hair. "Always remember that I love you, okay?"

"*No.*" Everett sobbed, shaking his head violently. "No, shut up, you're not dying! You can't, Rhys, you can't die on me! I won't let you—"

"Shh," Rhys whispered, smiling when Everett pulled back, letting him see his face again. He reached up to wipe away a tear on his cheek with his thumb. Everett leaned into the touch, whimpering, his own hands coming up to clutch Rhys's. "Just let me go. It's my t-time."

Everett took a sharp intake of breath, shaking his head again as if steeling himself for something.

"No," he said forcefully, standing up suddenly, leaving Rhys to whine pathetically at the loss of his touch, his warmth, reaching out for him as he walked away toward the door.

"E-Everett, where are you going?" Rhys panicked, crying dry tears as he helplessly watched Everett pull on his winter boots. He was going outside. Rhys's weak heart picked up the pace in pure panic. "Everett, *no*, what are you doing? Why are you going outside? You'd die out there!"

Everett had the gall to smile—that son of a fucking bitch—as he opened the door, letting a violent, freezing whir of snow and wind inside. He took one step out, then another, ignoring Rhys's hoarse screams, only turning back to utter a single phrase.

"I love you too, Rhys."

And with that, he closed the door and disappeared into the swirling snow, purpose unknown, taking Rhys's heart out into the cold with him.

Chapter Ten

Rhys softly hummed a nameless tune under his breath to the beat of his wooden knitting needles clacking against each other dully. He'd been working on the blanket for a couple of hours now, having not been able to sleep all night. After a while of tossing and turning, he'd given up, instead deciding to use the time productively in a way that wouldn't risk waking his slumbering love.

The project idea had been sparked a few days ago when Everett complained about the temperature at night. It was still a bit cold, only a month or two into spring, but significantly warmer than winter had been. All of the furs Rhys had stocked were thick and warm, too much so for the season. Remembering that he had a few large skeins of wool yarn, he'd come up with the idea to knit a blanket that would be comfy but wouldn't trap a lot of heat from their bodies pressed up against each other. He hoped Everett would love it, especially the light-pink hue that matched the little wildflowers that had begun to pop up around the garden beds.

It was also the same soft color of the sky when the sun eventually rose and filled the cabin with warm light filtering in through the linen curtains. The birds awakened with the sun, chirping and trilling a sweet, happy tune that almost harmonized with Rhys's. He was so glad winter was finally over, the long-awaited spring here to bless them with plentiful prey and the fields with bright-green grass and blooming flowers. Even after all these years, winter was still hard on him—spring could never come fast enough.

Every so often, he glanced up from his work and across the room to where Everett lay so peacefully on his side, his back to Rhys. Only his feet were visible, sticking out from underneath the thin fur blanket draped over his body. Rhys hoped his toes weren't getting cold from the slight chill in the room, or he wasn't overheating with his head under the blanket.

Movement from the corner of his eye brought his fond gaze over to the window in the kitchen. A blue jay had landed on the windowsill and peeked through the small opening between the two curtains. It flapped a wing as if in greeting, to which Rhys replied with a wave. Its wings were so pretty, a dazzling, vibrant blue. He'd never seen this species here before, since birds like these usually didn't stray so far from warmer climates, especially in this season. The old wooden chair groaned as he stood up to hurry across the room, eager to wake Everett to see this beautiful specimen. Though Rhys was hesitant to ruin his sleep, it was morning anyway, so it was only a matter of time before he would've woken up naturally from the light shining through the blanket.

"Everett," Rhys whispered with a smile on his face, hands reaching out to pull the blankets off of him. "Wake up, sleepyhead, there's a blue jay—wh-what the?"

Instead of Everett blinking sleepily up at him, his eyes were already wide open, unblinking, irises covered by the same thin layer of ice that covered his entire body like some sort of sick rendition of a cocoon. But Everett wasn't a butterfly, nor was he even fucking alive, his heart silent and still when Rhys checked for a pulse. Blue tinged his skin as if he'd been out in the cold for too long. But that was impossible. He hadn't been outside; he'd been here in bed the whole time. This couldn't have happened; there was no way Everett was dead.

"Everett!" Rhys screamed hoarsely in horror, hot tears falling onto his love's frozen face. The icy coating turned into sharp shards that dug into Rhys's palms as he hysterically grabbed at Everett's body—though it didn't hurt. He couldn't feel it, not when his heart was in way more pain. "No, Everett! You can't be—wake up! Wake up, Everett. You can't die. You can't leave me. You can't, you can't, I won't let you!"

He shook Everett's rigid body as if it could awaken him from a deep slumber, as if that was all this was, just any other normal morning. But it wasn't, far from it. It was a living nightmare, Rhys's worst dream come true. How long had he been knitting so peacefully while his love lay dead? How had he not noticed before?

"Everett!" He sobbed violently, collapsing to the floor with Everett's body falling with him, on top of him. "No, no, no, no!"

A drop of water fell onto his face, then two, then three. The ice was melting, as if Everett was crying, too, sobbing just as hard as Rhys was, mourning the loss of himself. Rhys sputtered when the drops kept coming, landing on his eyes, in his mouth, everywhere. It was too warm, wasn't even cold, and all he could see were Everett's frozen irises, so cold and dull and lifeless—

Rhys's own eyes snapped open.

For a moment, it was too blurry to see anything more than a vague, smudgy shadow looming over him. A muddled haze covered the whole world as if the ice on Everett's eyes had taken over Rhys's as well. No longer was he holding Everett's body in his arms, but something else was on top of him, holding him down, a heavy weight that had him panicking because he *couldn't fucking move.* He couldn't even voice his hysteria, throat choking on nothing, barely able to breathe. It was as if someone were sitting on his chest, knees pressing into his lungs, suffocating him. He blinked rapidly, the only part of his body he could control, his irises frantically darting back and forth, unseeing.

Though absolutely and utterly terrified and confused, somehow, he was sane enough to realize that the frozen, dead Everett had only been his fevered brain playing a sick trick on him. At the same time, he lacked enough sanity to discern if he was still stuck in a loop of nightmares or maybe some sort of sleep paralysis. He'd had a few episodes when he was younger, waking up trapped somewhere in the space between being asleep and awake, unable to move as demon-like creatures danced around his bed. But this—*this* was different. It had never felt so *real* before.

Liquid continued to drip onto his forehead, he realized belatedly. Drop after drop fell onto his face from a source unknown. *Warm* liquid. *Red* liquid. Like the drool of a beast that had just caught its prey, blood staining its saliva. It could've been Rhys's blood, but there was no way to tell if he was injured or not as he was completely numb from the neck down. He should've been worried about missing a limb or something. Though as his vision began to clear, there was something much more pressing on his mind.

Squinting hard, he almost recognized the dark silhouette above him. It wasn't a human; that he was sure of. It was something distinctly animal. Its teeth, long and sharp, could've sliced Rhys's neck open in mere seconds, tearing him to shreds before he could even blink in reaction. They couldn't belong to anything but a predator, a *wolf*.

A wolf with black fur, far larger than an ordinary wolf, paws almost disproportionately gigantic, like the prints he had come across so often. They pushed down against his chest with claws that could've definitely broken through the shirt and his skin with just a smidge more force. They could've scratched at him as if digging for his organs to feast on, as though he were nothing more than prey, a little lost deer. His stomach lurched as if to puke up what was left of his stomach acid, but nothing came out.

It was *him*, Rhys realized, eyes widening in unadulterated fear. The creature he'd tried to kill, with blood dripping from its intimidating, razor-sharp teeth, had returned for its revenge in one of his most vulnerable, weakest moments.

Adrenaline rushed to all of his numb limbs, filling them with blood in an attempt to fight or take flight from the angry beast. He thrashed under its hold, flailing pathetically, unable to escape. The wolf let out a noise, something that sounded like a mix between a snarling growl and a whine. Rhys screamed hoarsely in response, heart pumping like mad in his chest.

When its giant, blood-soaked snout leaned in close to his face, baring its teeth, Rhys thought it would finally end his misery. But it didn't bite at him as he expected. Instead, its deadly jaws opened wide to let its long, rough tongue slither out and lick Rhys's face from chin to forehead, coating him in another layer of putrid saliva.

He was still dreaming. He had to be dreaming—he *had* to be. In reality, there was no way he'd still be alive at this point, not when he was at the mercy of a bloodthirsty wolf.

A few long, tense moments passed before Rhys dared to peek his eyes open again. The wolf was still there, still whining like a kicked puppy, as if expecting something. Its eyes bored down into Rhys, so dark and imploring and— familiar, somehow.

They were shaped in such an alien but distinctly recognizable way, so sharp but also so delicate. Dark-brown irises burned with an intensity that could rival fire, sending shockwaves of heat through Rhys.

He *knew* those eyes.

He knew them because he'd fallen in love with them every day for an entire season, every day as autumn turned to winter, as everything around him died in the frost. At least this warmth was still alive, the flame refusing to be snuffed by the cold winter winds.

"E-*Everett*?" he rasped, reaching a shaky, weak hand up to card through the wolf's thick fur. "Is...that you?"

The wolf yipped softly and nodded its head way too humanlike. What a trippy nightmare this was. Rhys's fever must have really fucked him up if he was dreaming about Everett as a fucking sentient wolf, understanding human language. Its pink tongue lolled out of its mouth as if in a happy smile, somehow resembling Everett's own smile, so endearingly precious and cute Rhys couldn't help but giggle.

"You make a pretty wolf, Everett," he croaked out, barely audibly. "Too bad you aren't real though."

At that, Wolf-Everett shook his head with a bark and rested it on Rhys's chest. Rhys had to strain to look down at him, but he didn't mind, nor did he mind this dream one bit, now that he knew there was no need to be afraid anymore.

Though, he did remember why he was scared at first as he focused on the drying globs of blood staining the wolf's fur all over, like dyed streaks. "Why're you all bloody?"

Wolf-Everett whined again, head motioning over toward the right. Rhys followed his gaze and landed on an equally bloody, lifeless body by the door, one with a sizeable rack of antlers on its head—a buck with its neck ripped open, blood still dark red as it ruined Rhys's flooring.

Rhys chuckled breathlessly. "That's one hell of a kill, wolfy. Did ya take it down all by yourself?"

Wolf-Everett barked, his fluffy tail wagging furiously behind him, making Rhys grin as best he could with his lack of energy.

"What a good boy," he praised in a slurred voice, his weak fingers slowing in their petting without him realizing the extent of the exhaustion that crept back up on him. Rhys yawned, long and drawn out, eyes beginning to droop closed. "Y-you enjoy that dinner for me, okay?

I...I'm gonna take a nap, now, so go ahead and eat without me."

And with that, Rhys promptly passed out, despite Wolf-Everett's panicked barks of protest, dreaming of warmth instead of ice.

★

The next time, Rhys was sure he was awake.

Well, maybe. He might've been dead for all he knew. Honestly, he wasn't very religious, but if this was heaven, then perhaps he might consider believing in God. He lay on his mattress, which had been pulled to the floor to rest next to the fireplace with countless blankets and furs piled on top of him. His hunger pangs seemed to be gone, replaced with a pleasantly full belly. Rhys had no recollection of being moved here nor of eating, but who was he to complain when he was just so damn comfortable? The fireplace roared beside him, with several logs of firewood next to it—which, again, didn't make much sense since he swore they'd run out just before Everett had left.

Everett had left. Right. There was no way Rhys was still alive or awake because there Everett was, lying right next to him. He snored softly, his warm breath sending goose bumps down Rhys's body where his head was buried in the junction between Everett's neck and shoulders. He'd wrapped his long arms and legs around Rhys's body, clingy as ever. Rhys was 100 percent sure now that he was in yet another dream—one calling back a memory from the past, from the first few days of Everett's stay—since there was no discernable reason he'd be allowed through the gates of heaven with all of his sins on his back.

Rhys lifted his gaze to stare at Everett's sleeping, peaceful face, which scrunched up in protest when Rhys dared to poke at his slightly reddened nose. He missed his hallucination of Wolf-Everett, but this was just as good if not better, one he'd gladly have as his last sight before he inevitably passed away. Sure, it wasn't real—of course it wasn't; it couldn't be. It was just another dream. But anything was better than having that dreaded, horribly *real* memory of Everett walking out into the blizzard repeating over and over again until it turned Rhys mad with anguish. It was nice of his mind to conjure up such a comforting image instead of torturing itself.

"Pretty," Rhys murmured quietly to himself, voice raspy from sleep.

He gently stroked his thumb along the hard, sharp line of Everett's striking jaw. Moving slowly to savor the moment, he mapped out every curve of his face, from the small tuft of coiled hair at his widow's peak, to the barely-there divots of his dimpled cheeks, and to the soft, pillowy lips that parted open ever so slightly. Rhys hesitated to touch the foreign territory for a moment. But then he gave in to his desires, stroking the pads of his fingers across the warm flesh as would Everett's tongue after he'd finished eating. He giggled under his breath when he spotted a small dribble of drool at one corner, so comical yet so endearing, even in this dream world.

Despite that, though, Everett's lips were incredibly inviting, begging even, for Rhys to caress them in a different way, with his own. Rhys immediately shoved the thought from his mind, but after some deliberation, he wondered what harm there could be, this one time, to experience what it felt like to kiss Everett. It would be his only chance to do so, after all. And though the idea of stealing a kiss while Everett couldn't consent wouldn't be something Rhys would condone in the real world, this was still a dream. *Everett* was still a dream, and dreams of one's own weren't beholden to morals.

Everett's hot breath ghosted along Rhys's skin, deceptively real as Rhys slowly leaned in close, sucking in his own nervous breath with their faces only millimeters apart. It felt wrong—yet so *right* at the same time, so right there was no way he could've held himself back from fluttering his eyes shut and closing the rest of the distance between them to plant his chapped, cold lips against Everett's warm ones.

It wasn't Rhys's first kiss—far from it—but it was almost as if it were, filled with warm tingles that had him giggling against Everett's lips. For a moment, he felt twelve years old again, kissing his crush behind the slide to hide from the recess monitor, a hopeless romantic of a delinquent.

Too much time had passed since Rhys was this close to someone, felt this way toward someone. He was sure he'd never been half as in love with anyone as he was with Everett, loving him with his entire being and soul. He would never feel Everett's love in return, not now when everything was but a dream, when the real world beyond had crumbled into ruins. Now, though, kissing Dream-Everett was enough and far more than Rhys deserved.

Though the kiss was meant to be chaste, nothing more than a peck, Everett seemed to think otherwise, responding to Rhys even in his sleep. Rhys squeaked when the soft lips melted against his own, starting at a slow, gentle pace, a push and pull he quickly became lost in, forgetting where they were, who he was, everything, his mind only filled with Everett, Everett, *Everett*.

It was a dream; it wasn't real. Everett wasn't actually kissing him of his own volition, but Rhys allowed himself to indulge in his fantasies anyway. The sounds of their lips' embrace filled the small room along with the crackling of the fireplace. Rhys's small mewls and Everett's breathy groans seemed a bit lewd in combination with the wet slip and slide of their tongues. The situation only grew more heady and desperate when large hands pawed at Rhys's waist—though when he heard his name whispered like a prayer into the night, his eyes flew open.

Everett was awake now, blushing furiously as Rhys pulled back from the kiss to meet two sleepy, dark eyes, blinking dreamily open to greet him.

"Hey there, pretty," Rhys whispered, a small smile pulling at his cheeks as he watched Everett shoot up quickly from the bed, eyes wide and mouth gaping like a fish. "Why do you look like you've seen a ghost, hmm? Come lie back down with me; I'm still so tired—"

"D-did you just *kiss* me?" Everett blurted out, as still as a statue before his eyes suddenly widened so much they threatened to pop out from their sockets, all sleepiness lost and replaced with utter glee. "Wait, holy shit, you're awake! Rhys—oh my fucking hell, thank god it worked! I saved you! Hah, fuck you, death. You can't take my Rhys away from me!"

The exclamation took Rhys by surprise, and he furrowed his brows in confusion. Why was Dream-Everett reacting like this? It was a dream, and shouldn't this figure of Rhys's imagination have been following what *he* desired? What was he talking about, with all of this "saving him" crap? Saving him from what?

Rhys blinked rapidly, heart beginning to seize in panic now that the happy haze of the kiss had lifted, leaving him once again to deal with the fear of his impending death. He couldn't waste his time here, not when any second, his body would finally perish in the real world, snuffing out this once beautiful dream into darkness forever.

"What the fuck are you talking about— Actually, you know what? Let's just go back to kissing, o-okay? Let me enjoy this dream while I still can, please? I-I don't have that much time—"

Before Rhys could ramble any further, with tears gathering in his eyes, Everett carefully lifted a hand to cradle his head ever so gently.

"Damn it. *Fuck*. You should be better by now. You're still feverish and delusional, aren't you?" Everett sighed. "Rhys, you're not dreaming, okay? You've been asleep for eight days. You woke up a few times but...not really. It wasn't you—you weren't all there like now. You're *alive*, and I-I saved you. I worked so hard, but I thought I'd lost you—" Everett choked up, his big eyes shiny with real, genuine tears.

It wasn't a dream.

"I...*Everett*..."

Without thinking, Rhys burrowed himself into Everett's chest, sobbing with all the newfound energy his body had to give. He was embraced in return, so carefully, as if he had fragile bones that would snap easily. Hands stroked his back up and down, the only sensation his mind could focus on.

Rhys didn't know how it was even possible that Everett was here—he'd seen Everett walk out into that nasty blizzard with his very own eyes. There was no way he should've been able to survive the wretched winds and frigid temperatures that should've stricken him with frostbite and frozen him from the inside out, just like in Rhys's first dream. It was impossible. Yet here Everett was, a survivor of the winter's rage, a battle he hadn't even needed to engage in.

"I-I thought you died," Rhys wailed, "You left me, Everett, *abandoned* me—"

"N-*no*," Everett urged, his arms tightening around Rhys. "*No*, that's not it, Rhys, you don't understand. I didn't abandon you. I would *never*."

Rhys peeled himself back enough to look up at Everett through damp eyelashes, eyes pink and puffy from crying so hard. "Then why, Everett, *why*? Why did you l-leave me? *Why*?"

Everett couldn't seem to meet his tear-filled gaze, eyes looking anywhere but down at Rhys, as if ashamed. "I had to," he said through gritted teeth. "I needed to do something to save you, *anything*. I couldn't just sit around and let you die—"

"Yes, yes you could have!" Rhys screamed, making Everett flinch. "I'd have rather died here with you than alone! What if you never came back, Everett? What if the last I ever saw you was when you walked out that door? What if I died before you could make it back from whatever you thought was so much more important, huh?"

Clenching his eyes closed, the veins in Everett's forehead stood out. "Please stop—"

Rhys knew he should've focused on the elation of finding each other alive, yet there was no holding back his grief, his sadness, his anger.

"How could you?" he said, voice trembling. "How could you walk out that door and leave me behind? Right after I poured my heart out to you, told you I *loved* you. Did you even mean it when you said you loved me back? Look at me, Everett—"

A violent snarl ripped deep from within Everett's chest, so loud the vibrations jarred Rhys's frail body like an earthquake. A sound so terrifying, so bone-chilling, Rhys's entire body froze all at once, his mouth snapping shut, eyes growing wide in disbelief that his Everett had somehow made that noise.

"You can tell me so many things, and I won't fucking care," Everett sneered, his voice edged with a rumble that had Rhys's blood running cold. "But don't you fucking dare imply that I don't love you! I would die for you with a smile on my face. I would protect you with my last dying breath—with pleasure because you are mine! You are my pack. You are *mine*, and I have to protect you!"

Tears streaked down Everett's red face, now so sad yet so angry. Rhys was conflicted, wanting to wipe the tears away and cower back in fear. He couldn't run away, not with his weak body, not when Everett had transformed into something entirely inhuman right before his very eyes.

"How dare *you*, Rhys? How dare you accuse me of abandoning you, when all I was doing was risking my fucking life for you, to *save* you, to bring you back food so you wouldn't starve to death? And you know what? You're right; I *did* almost die out there, but it was worth it, worth *you*, and I'd do it again for you a thousand times more, whether you approve of it or not, because I love you, Rhys. I fucking love you, so don't you dare tell me otherwise."

Rhys didn't know what to say. Honestly, even if he did, he wasn't sure he'd even be able to speak. His mouth was as dry as if he'd eaten a handful of gritty sand. His heart thumped through his chest like a rabbit whose leg had been caught in a snare.

Everett was still speaking, but Rhys was no longer listening, the growls fading into a low background hum. Unable to hear, he could only stare up at Everett's furious face, his narrowed eyes and tightened, clenched jawline, and his rapidly moving mouth—and his teeth. His sharp, protruding canines, to be exact.

How had he never noticed that before? Over the last couple of months, he'd spent hours upon hours gazing upon Everett's face—while he slept, laughed, talked, ate—but he'd always had normal human teeth, not these animal like razor blades. His mind had to be playing another trick on him, but he wasn't sure what to think anymore. He squeezed his eyes shut, but they were still fucking there when he opened them, glinting mockingly. The teeth didn't match Everett at all, looking completely out of place yet, at the same time, perfectly accompanying the terrifying snarls and growls as if some wolf had taken over Everett's body—

The wolf. The image of canine eyes and sharp teeth, dark fur and a long snout flashed in his mind. It was just a dream. But...*this* was undeniably real, and so was Everett. Rhys's dreams had melded with reality into one giant clusterfuck.

There was only one explanation for it, and no matter how silly it seemed to come to this conclusion, Rhys finally felt as though he could see clearly for the first time in weeks—and feel the downright *terror*. How could he not be terrified when he was trapped in the arms of a fucking *werewolf*?

The longer Rhys stared up at Everett's face, the softer it became. His growls had subsided into huffs. He stopped speaking, fury melting second by second. He'd no doubt registered the terror playing across Rhys's features, from his wide eyes, to his clammy skin, to his tensed body ready to bolt at any second, to his throat as he gulped heavily.

"I...oh my god, Rhys, I'm so sorry. I didn't mean to lose my t-temper," Everett said, tripping over his words.

He went to touch Rhys's cheek, but Rhys flinched away from his touch, eyes slamming shut in anticipation of being mauled by this...creature. Everett frowned, slowly bringing his arm back.

"Rhys, please don't be scared of me. I—"

"Everett," Rhys interrupted as forcefully as he could manage, although it came out a bit squeakier than he'd hoped, his entire body shaking, and not from the cold this time. "You're...what *are* you?"

Everett was taken aback by the question, his own eyes widening, irises darting around. "Uh...what?" He laughed nervously, forced and too loud. "What do you mean, 'what am I'? I'm Everett!"

"*No*. No, Everett. What. Are. You. What are *those*?" Rhys pointed at Everett's teeth. "What were those...noises you were making, huh? And don't you lie to me! *What are you*? Because you certainly aren't fucking human!"

Everett's hands flew up to feel around his mouth, his body jolting ramrod straight when his fingers grazed along the points of his canines, so sharp they nicked his skin and a small bit of blood trickled down his hand. He gasped at the red liquid as if frightened of it just as much as Rhys was, if not more.

"I-I," he whispered, eyes flickering between his wound and Rhys, who had begun to scoot back away from him. "Rhys, I...I swear I was going to tell you—"

"What? That you're a fucking *werewolf*?" Rhys scoffed, not wanting to hear Everett spout bullshit any longer. "What the hell, Everett! That's not something you just...hide from a person, especially the person who has been housing you, feeding you, taking care of you, *loving* you!"

"It's not like it's that easy to tell you I'm a wolf shifter!" Everett shot back as he stood, now looming over Rhys. He paced back and forth, his hands tightly fisted at his side. "You hate wolves, Rhys! You despise them! You tried to kill one even...tried to kill *me*!"

It all made sense now. Why Everett, of all things, was the prey in his wolf trap. Now that he thought about it, Rhys's previous theories about him running away from his family, a cult, or a sex trafficking ring seemed more like fiction than Everett being a monster out of fairytales. How likely would it have been for a runaway to find Rhys's tiny section of the backwoods among the hundreds of miles of forest on that specific day *and* step straight into his trap? One in millions. How likely would it have been for the wolf—*were*wolf—that'd been stalking Rhys for months to follow the scent trail of the bait and get caught? A hundred and ten percent.

"It was *you*, wasn't it? The bastard wolf who was stealing all my kills?"

Everett had the gall to look offended at the words. He had no right, not after lying to Rhys for so long. "I wasn't *stealing* them—"

"Don't act like you don't know what the word 'stealing' means, Everett, because I clearly remember teaching it to you when we played Monopoly," Rhys snapped. "What else would you call it then, when you deliberately waited until the prey I shot ran out of view so you could snatch it up before I could catch up? I shot them all first! It's not like you never had your own chance to kill them fair and square. That's stealing, and it's not fucking right!"

"Rhys, wait—"

"Is that why you decided to stay with me, huh?" Rhys continued, not caring that Everett appeared to be about to cry again. Rhys wasn't falling for it this time. "Couldn't hunt for your damn self so you thought you'd trick me into helping a fake homeless kid?"

Rhys seethed, his blood boiling in his veins. He wanted to scream, to get up and punch the shit out of Everett for taking advantage of him, for making him look foolish this whole time. He wanted to kick him out into the blizzard and let him die, but all he could do with his weak body was hope his words hit just as hard as his fists would.

Everett sniffled and visibly deflated, his eyes glued to the bloodstain on the floor. He was silent for a long moment, so long Rhys was about to start his rant again until Everett knelt in front of him and spoke in a quiet, hurt whisper.

"Rhys, I-I got kicked out of my pack. Got run out of the territory last spring."

Rhys cocked an eyebrow. "Okay? And?"

"*And* you're right. I stole your prey because I couldn't do it myself. Spent months alone and was barely able to hunt rabbits, not a single deer. You're *right*, okay? I-I'm a fucking stealing bastard wolf who can't hunt for shit. They never taught me how, always preferred my other siblings to go out on hunts with them while I was left to pick at the *bones* just because I was the runt, not worth using resources on. And then they kicked me out because I flirted with one of the neighboring pack's sons when he came looking for my sisters during the mating season—"

Everett growled under his breath and shook his head. "It's no excuse for my behavior toward you, though, no matter how desperate and starving I was. I know it was wrong to steal from you. That's why I've tried so hard from the start to be useful to you. I wasn't even planning on staying any longer than a few weeks but I...I fell in *love* with you, Rhys. I fell in love with everything about you, even what you may think are your flaws—I love them. And I couldn't just leave, not when you were so alone. You act like you're so tough, but you need someone here with you, to care for you, to love you like you deserve—and you deserve so much love, Rhys, *so much*. It was never about taking advantage of you. I would *never*."

Everett held their eye contact steady, making Rhys feel as though his expression was being desperately searched. And Everett must've not found what he was looking for because he let out a long sigh and hung his head.

"I understand if you don't believe me though. I was the one stealing your kills for months, the one who put you in this position of almost dying of starvation. I can never forgive myself for always being such a fucking *wimp*."

Everett paused to laugh bitterly as tears fell from his face onto the floor. "You know, I could've gone out to hunt weeks ago. I have better senses than you, so with all of the hunting knowledge you gave me, I would've been able to hunt down a deer for us just like that one. Except, it would have to be in my wolf form, which meant I'd have to tell you. I knew if I told you I'm a wolf, *the wolf*, you'd hate me, kick me out, or even fucking kill me. I was scared, Rhys.

"But, when you told me you love me...I thought that would mean if I revealed my wolf side, you might've been able to look past it and still love me and forgive me. But maybe...I was wrong. Maybe your love for me isn't enough to outweigh your anger and fear. So, now that I've succeeded in saving your life...if you want to, you can kill me, and I won't put up a fight."

Rhys didn't know how to react, how to feel, not when Everett was begging on his knees for his forgiveness and understanding. He wanted to believe his words, he really did, but it was almost impossible for him to look past the lies, even if they were supposedly told out of good intention. There was no way for him to know whether Everett wasn't still lying straight through his teeth, even now. Rhys had been lied to so much in the past, been tricked and made a fool of.

How could he trust Everett after this? How could he look at him in the same way, now that it'd been revealed he was part animal? Would he someday turn on Rhys out of instinctual, feral anger and rip him to shreds? Was he only taking care of Rhys because he wanted to fatten him up to eat come spring?

But at the same time, how could Rhys just forget and deny his love for Everett?

Lies were still lies; stealing was still stealing—yet at the same time, love was still love, and his love for Everett was something he would never be able to erase. So what if he had lied and stolen? So what if he was a fucking werewolf? *So fucking what?* Everett wasn't his parents, his exes, or the no-good world Rhys had left behind; he was only Everett, Rhys's first ever real love. No one had ever done this much for Rhys before, gone to such an effort to prove the extent of their love selflessly without asking anything in return. How could he push him away? How could he hold a grudge over him? How could he vilify him out of his own past trauma? He *couldn't*—and he didn't want to. He wanted Everett, with his lies, stealing, wolfyness, and all.

"This is hard for me, Everett." Rhys sighed. "I'm definitely not going to kill you, so shut up about that. But…I don't…know what to do. I've never been in love with a werewolf before—"

"You still love me?" Everett blurted out and then slapped a hand over his mouth as if he didn't mean to ask that.

Rhys giggled softly. Yup, he was still very much enamored with Everett, even now. "Of course I do. You think my love is that fragile? Because it isn't, and that's what scares me— I still love you, even when you steal and lie and terrify me. Like what the hell? Is there something wrong with me? Jesus Christ, I'm in love with a fucking werewolf like I'm in goddamn *Twilight* or something. I'm still not convinced I'm not still dreaming right now. I thought you liked women this entire time!"

"Not a single thing is wrong with you, except maybe being oblivious, thinking I like women. I thought it was pretty obvious that I was and am attracted to *you*." Everett laughed in disbelief. He dared to hesitantly reach out his hand again to touch Rhys's shoulder, a small smile rising when his affection was accepted this time. "And you're not dreaming; I promise this is very, very real. And so is my love for you."

"Shut up. That's so cheesy!"

Everett's smile widened as he pinched Rhys's pouty bottom lip. "*You* shut up; you know you like it," he teased. "But...does that mean you forgive me? A-and still want me here? Because I totally understand if you want me to fuck off forever—"

"Just shut up, and come kiss me already."

And he did. Everett fell into Rhys's embrace easily, letting their lips meld together for the second time that night, holding each other so close it almost hurt. It wasn't as passionate as the first, but perfectly slow, letting them get lost in the moment. Rhys didn't even mind it when he felt Everett's canines scrape ever so slightly against his lips, no longer afraid of them, only grinning into the kiss like an idiot.

Eventually, their lips parted, but their embrace didn't. Everett held Rhys like they were never going to see each other again—and based on how this almost had been the case, the feeling made a lot of sense. Rhys hugged him back just as tight, arms wrapped around his torso like his life depended on it.

Silence filled the cabin for a while, save for the occasional sniffles and soft, pleased sighs, as well as the crackling of the fireplace. The silence wasn't awkward or uncomfortable, as there were no other words needed. Rhys's feelings were still such a jumbled mess, but this moment was quite welcome, leaving his worries for another day, another time. In his lover's arms, he had a safe place, a comfortable haven, where he could purely enjoy the love they shared.

He couldn't really deny it anymore, could he? The things he felt were too real. The food in his belly, Everett's very warm and very alive brown eyes, sparkling with the trillions of stars of the pure and unrelenting love they shared. As impossible as it all seemed, it was all too real to be a dream. Rhys really had woken up. And Everett had, by some miracle, found his way back to his side.

It was all so overwhelming that he couldn't help but tremble slightly. Rhys was incredibly relieved. This lifestyle had worked well for him but for one flaw: his loneliness. The second he'd found his remedy, it had been ripped away from him so violently. But now, Everett was back, and there was absolutely no way Rhys would ever let him go again.

"You called me 'my Rhys' earlier, hmm?" he whispered.

Everett's posture tensed slightly.

"W-well...yeah. Because you're mine," he stammered, nuzzling Rhys's hair. "Right?"

Rhys's face warmed, even though it wasn't himself he was trying to fluster. "I mean…if you want me to be," he murmured, wringing his fingers nervously.

"Of course I do," Everett rushed out with zero hesitation. "And I want to be yours as well, if you'll have me."

"Of course I will." Rhys smiled, tilting his head up to plant a kiss on Everett's nose. "We belong to each other."

Chapter Eleven

Things seemed to look promising for the couple's hope of surviving the rest of the long winter together.

The deer Everett had dragged home was a well-fed buck with plenty of meat on its bones. How he had even managed to track down such a magnificent beast floored Rhys at first since the deer were supposed to have migrated down the mountain to the valley. Somehow, Everett had not only managed to trudge those long, arduous miles in the blizzard, but also found the buck, which had been injured already. He'd killed it and lugged the carcass back to the cabin all by himself in his starvation-weakened state. Everett attributed this to Rhys's amazing hunting lessons, though Rhys knew it had more to do with the werewolf's superhuman abilities.

Only days later, the blizzard tapered off into gentle snow showers, as if somehow knowing its goal had been completed when the couple had admitted their feelings to each other. Though the snow was still a couple of feet deep with ice hiding underneath, it was finally safe again to venture outside the cabin and revel in the calmer winds and clearer skies, admiring the beautiful landscape they called home.

However, Rhys was unable to enjoy their bounty of food or join Everett as the wolf happily romped through the snow, clearing pathways and hunting rabbits. It sounded like a simple task, to recover from starvation; all he needed was to eat and he'd be better in no time...right?

Wrong. His recovery was more like downright *hell*.

While Everett's magical werewolf powers had allowed him to heal almost entirely in just two weeks, Rhys's weak human body took three painful months, which was completely unfair and rigged.

Despite Rhys being incredibly hungry and the venison smelling absolutely delicious, his traitorous stomach wouldn't keep down much of anything. It rejected food for weeks; as it had gone so long without any, it didn't recognize nutrients anymore. Vomiting so often had caused Rhys to become disgusted by even the idea of food, though Everett still forced him to eat. More often than not, Rhys would find himself slumped over a bucket filled with his own puke, the putrid taste of bile in his mouth and Everett's comforting hand stroking his back.

Though he desperately wanted to escape the claustrophobic confines of the cabin and run outside, Rhys remained bedridden for two months. During his period of starvation, his body had begun to consume itself, leaving him with little muscle mass and fat reserves. His limbs, thin and brittle, threatened to snap when he so much as put on his clothes in the morning. He couldn't walk on his own, with his legs as thin as his arms, and needed Everett to either carry him everywhere or eventually be used as a human crutch.

The cold was twice as brutal on him without enough mass to keep him warm, so he always lay by the fire wrapped in as many blankets as possible, usually with Everett cozied up by his side. When they weren't cuddling, Everett took care of the outside chores, from clearing the snow to catching rabbits and deer. Rhys could only watch from the window with a pout, not even able to sit out on the porch thanks to the nipping cold.

The hardest part of recovery was the effect starvation had on his brain. Rhys had potential nerve damage that caused searing pains to shoot down his limbs like lightning when he moved too fast. And most nights, Rhys relived the nightmare he'd had the day Everett came back, dreaming of finding his love frozen and dead. He'd wake up in a cold sweat and sobbing, desperately holding Everett as if afraid he'd disappear into the cold again, leaving him to starve and die alone. Everett could only watch with tears of his own, whispering reassurances that he'd never, *ever* leave like that again.

They both worried that Rhys would need to be taken down to a hospital, but thankfully, it never got to that point. As the months passed, his stomach slowly learned to tolerate simple, small meals such as bland broths with small chunks of meat, carrots, and potatoes—the backwoods equivalent of chicken noodle soup. By the end of the third month, Rhys was overjoyed to be able to chow down ravenously on big plates of venison steaks, almost as if he were the wolf instead. Mass eventually returned to his body, with Rhys feeling stronger each day. During their nightly cuddle sessions, Everett took immense pleasure in Rhys gaining his weight back, nuzzling against the subtle layer of fat that now covered his ribs. Though Rhys still experienced the occasional nightmares, pains, and muscle weakness, they were both relieved to see his gradual recovery in time for spring, which had just begun.

Now that he was significantly stronger, Everett allowed himself to shift more often, no longer afraid Rhys would need his human form twenty-four-seven. Rhys found himself, most mornings, waking up to a gigantic fluffy wolf taking up half of his bed. And if sometimes he woke up pinned to the wall, he really didn't mind it.

Wolf-Everett was an even better cuddle buddy than his human counterpart, warmer than any fur blanket could ever be, so Rhys never complained unless Everett also decided he needed a face licking to go along with the cuddles.

One night, the two of them lay by the fireplace, Rhys reading the first *Harry Potter* book aloud, petting the wolf and reveling in the softness after giving him a well-needed bath. Earlier that day, they'd gone out to set up new rabbit snares and collect firewood. But, before they returned inside, Everett had decided to shift and roll around on the ground in protest. He'd ended up becoming quite dirty with mud and snow, much to Rhys's annoyance. After wrestling the yelping, struggling, overgrown puppy into the bathtub, without getting mud all over the cabin, Rhys discovered his fur was actually a very pleasant texture when properly taken care of—and when not reeking of *wet dog*.

The fire snapped and crackled, a log crumbling as it fell into the embers, burning into charcoal. Everett's ear flickered at the noise, and he opened an eye to check for danger before closing it once more. Rhys couldn't help but giggle at the canine's protective, jumpy antics. Though, he had to admit it was comforting to know if there was any impending danger to them, Everett would always be there on the defense.

"Everett." Rhys sighed with a small, fond smile, scratching behind the wolf's ear. "Why are you so vigilant? It's just the fireplace; it can't hurt me. Just relax, okay?"

Everett's leg, as always, kicked as he melted into a big puddle of fluff and warmth. His jaw dropped open, allowing a floppy pink tongue to loll out, his eyes closed tight happily. He rolled over, showing off his belly, wagging his tail so fast it thumped loudly every time it made contact with the floor.

At this display, Rhys paused in his ministrations, his eyes widening. Sure, he'd cuddled with the wolf more times than he could count by now, but this was the first time he had ever been granted access to belly rubs. The wolf did technically have the mind of a human, *Everett's* mind, but the significance of what this show of vulnerability meant in the canine world had his heart stuttering in his chest. Rhys had never owned a dog, but he was well aware of their behavior from his biology books, and "belly up" was either a sign of submission or trust.

"You...want belly rubs?" Rhys asked quietly, hand hovering hesitantly over the wolf.

Wolf-Everett nodded and stretched, exposing his belly even more, now completely on display. From his body language, it was evident there was no way for Rhys to refuse. The message was clear.

Tentatively, Rhys gave in, pressing a hand against the soft, fluffy wolf tummy. He braced himself for anything, really. A snarl. A growl. A flinch. Being torn to shreds.

No. Nothing but the content sigh of a very happy wolf, whose tail wagged excitedly. Allowing his shoulders to fall to a semi relaxed state, Rhys rubbed the wolf's stomach, appreciating the warmth and the vulnerable state Everett had put himself in. The more Rhys thought about it, the more he found himself becoming just a touch choked up. This was a display of something so pure and wholesome, something Rhys could only call *trust*. Something he struggled with himself, clearly.

Tears welled up in his eyes as he continued rubbing the wolf's tummy, smiling uncontrollably to the point that it might've looked crazed. Wolf-Everett reveled in the attention, tail wagging relentlessly, creating a rhythmic beat that resonated throughout the cabin.

"Silly puppy," Rhys cooed, putting down the book to wipe away his tears. "You like belly rubs, don't you?"

Wolf-Everett yipped happily in response, enjoying the petting for a few more minutes until he flipped himself over onto four paws. Caging Rhys beneath him, he licked at his face, replacing the tear tracks with his sticky saliva, making the human squawk and squirm away.

"Gross, wolf spit!" Rhys fake-gagged, swatting the chuffing wolf away. "Stop it, stop it! I need to finish reading that chapter!"

Everett rolled his eyes and gave a sassy little huff before settling back down on the floor, resuming their cuddle and reading session.

The two of them easily ended up spending the next few hours this way, enjoying both the warmth of the fire and each other. Giddy and tired, Rhys didn't end up falling asleep in their bed yet awoke in it somehow come morning. He turned over onto his side to look upon Everett's sleeping form, with the faint memory of warm, strong arms carrying him as if he weighed nothing, and soft lips pressing against his forehead.

★

The sun rose, sending gentle pink rays that graced every surface of the cabin. It painted the sky with scarlet and golden oil paints, gently blended across a still dark canvas. As always, Rhys awakened with the sun, sitting up and rubbing at his crusty eyes with a mighty yawn. He looked out the window next to him, a small smile curling the corners of his lips at the scene outside. Though spring's slight increase in temperature was already upon them, a good foot of unmelted snow still sparkled and glimmered. Almost blinding, the sunlight bounced off the fluffy blanket that covered the landscape in white, save for the paths Everett had cleared. Rhys wanted to check their rabbit traps, but for now, he remained stuck in the pleasant haze of sleep, appreciating how the view looked more like a painting than real life.

Eventually, he began to long for a different kind of beauty, and his gaze strayed over his shoulder to where Everett lay. Yet, he wasn't there.

In his stead, Rhys found a rabbit.

A *dead* rabbit, blood crusted throughout its fur, eyes opened wide in fear, staring right back at him, causing him to scream in shock and horror.

In an instant, Everett came running up from the cellar, snarling fiercely, ready to defend Rhys from whatever danger had caused him to be so terrified. But when his quick scan of the room found nothing of concern, a worried whine replaced his growling.

"What's wrong? Why did you scream?" he asked, kneeling beside Rhys, who had thrown himself on the floor as far away from the bed as he could.

Rhys furiously gestured over to the bloody, lifeless corpse. "Can you not see that...thing? It's *dead*! Why the *fuck* is there a dead rabbit in my bed? Get it out of here, oh my god, it's going to stain the blankets!"

Everett's eyebrows furrowed, gaze flickering back and forth between Rhys and the rabbit, before his eyes widened in realization. He laughed nervously, rubbing at the back of his neck.

"Oh, that. Do...do you n-not like it?" he asked sheepishly. "I'm sorry about all of the blood... I tried catching it with one of your snares first, but it wasn't exactly working, so I had to chase it down myself. It's nice, r-right? Good for frying? And a nice, soft pelt? Which would be small, I know, but I didn't have enough time to hunt for a deer."

Rhys blinked rapidly, his groggy mind reeling as it tried to understand what the actual *fuck* was going on right now. "Wait, wait, wait. Are you saying that...*you* put this thing here?"

There was an awkward pause before Everett replied, "Y-yeah..." Everett looked at his feet. "I hunted it down while you were sleeping. Is...that a bad thing? Because that's totally fine if you don't like it. It's small anyway. I can take it away a-and go catch you something else, whatever you want. Another deer? Some fish? I can even get a bear for you. It'll be hard, but I'll do anything for you, so just say the word and I'll—"

"But *why*?" Rhys interrupted with a squawk. He wasn't even upset about the rabbit anymore—it was the fact that Everett, yet again, had left him alone. "Everett, why the fuck would you go out hunting by yourself in the middle of the night? I thought we said no leaving for stupid reasons anymore! Are you trying to make me sick with worry again? You could have waited until I woke up so I could come with you."

Everett winced as if the words had physically hurt him, whimpering quietly. "It wasn't for a *stupid* reason," he defended in a grumbly tone, twiddling his thumbs. "And it isn't like I could have taken you with me. That would just ruin it. How am I supposed to surprise you with a courting gift if it isn't a surprise anymore?"

Rhys was raring and ready to argue back, but all his anger dissipated as quickly as it had started at the sad, disappointed look on Everett's face, almost as if he might cry.

"Courting gift?" Rhys asked slowly. He'd heard the word "courting" before in medieval romance stories, the old-timey term for dating. "What do you mean? Don't you mean dating?"

Everett's face flushed bright red. "I-I...I don't know what dating is, um... Forget I said anything! It's weird, I know. Just forget about it, p-please."

Rhys snorted loudly. Everett was adorable; he couldn't deny it, even when he'd been upset at him literally seconds ago. Everything about the werewolf was adorable, really. Rhys sometimes forgot Everett was very socially inexperienced in the human sense of the word, specifically when it came to romance, or anything of the sort, only having knowledge of the way of wild wolves. And this—the rabbit, the courting gift—must've been a part of that.

He was a bit miffed that this entire time he thought he and Everett had been on the same page in terms of them dating, but then again, relationship labels didn't matter—only feelings did.

"Everett," Rhys said softly, raising a hand to caress the side of his face. "Dating is when two people with romantic feelings decide they want to be exclusive, which means they don't want to be romantic with other people. It's similar to courting; dating couples also give each other gifts. But there are other things you can give me or do for me besides putting dead creatures on my bed."

Everett tilted his head slightly to the side, a confused expression knitting his thick brows together.

"Other ways? It's tradition. I don't think you understand. I—" Everett sighed. "Let's just drop it. Let me...let me get you breakfast, okay?"

"Okay, okay, I'll drop it," Rhys said, lightly chuckling under his breath. "Let me get dressed, and I'll be right with you."

Everett nodded, his cheeks matching the scarlet dawn shining in through the window. As Rhys stretched out his back, Everett snatched up the limp rabbit carcass and spun around on his heel to scurry to the kitchen.

The second Everett turned his back, Rhys shook his head slowly. Everett really was like an overgrown puppy, like ones Rhys had seen on Reddit that brought dead squirrels and mice to their frightened owners as if they were an extravagant gift.

He sent one last furtive glare over at the little red stain on his favorite blanket—*that's never going to come out, damn it*—before shuffling over to his dresser, shivering in his boxers. He didn't need his thick sweatpants and sweaters when sleeping next to Everett's space-heater body, but once he forced himself out of bed, the cold hit him like a truck. Thankfully, when he waddled out to join Everett in the kitchen, dressed in three layers, he was pleased to see the fire roaring healthily with a pot of tea boiling over the flames, ready to warm him up.

The rabbit soothed as well. Rhys fried up the lean meat after Everett had skinned and butchered it, creating a lovely, filling meal that started off the day just right, redeeming itself after his little...scare...from earlier. Rhys still felt bad about freaking out so much over a little thing. It wasn't the first time he'd seen a dead animal, of course, and it certainly wasn't the goriest one. Sue him—he was tired and startled!

He still didn't understand why Everett had killed the poor bunny in the first place, or what he meant by "courting gift." He'd called it tradition, but what the hell did Rhys know about werewolf traditions? Nothing. He knew *nothing*, though he assumed it was an important gesture by how stubborn Everett had been over pleasing him with his kill, probably more important than a regular gift. He'd been so upset when Rhys seemed to reject it— *Oh god*.

He stopped chewing. What if he was wrong, thinking that courting was similar to dating? What if werewolf courting was much more serious? What if it was something akin to a fucking *proposal*? A proposal that he had rejected so brutally.

"E-Everett," he started after swallowing the half-chewed piece of meat. "I know you're too embarrassed to talk about it, but please tell me... Were you trying to, um, propose to me with that rabbit, or something?"

Everett blinked. "Propose? What's that?"

Now it was Rhys's turn to be embarrassed—fuck, he might have assumed wrongly. Why would Everett ever want to propose to his dumb ass? Just because he loved him didn't mean he wanted to marry him.

"U-uh." He focused on stabbing another piece of meat with his fork. "A proposal...um... It's a thing that humans do when they want to, er, ask someone to marry them."

Again, Everett blinked. "Marry? What? Rhys, I don't understand—"

"Just tell me what the fucking rabbit meant already, oh my god!"

A pregnant silence filled the room, and Rhys promptly slapped a hand over his mouth. Wow, how subtle. Now he'd gone and made Everett uncomfortable again. Another example of why he'd make one shitty husband.

Everett put down his fork and squirmed in his seat, looking extremely uncomfortable. Another few minutes passed before he spoke up.

"You're going to think I'm dumb."

"No, I won't," Rhys said firmly. "*Never*, Everett; you're not dumb. And you don't have to tell me if you don't want to, okay?"

"I... It's not that I don't want to. I'm just..." Everett sighed. "It was a courting gift, Rhys. Courting gifts are...what a wolf shifter gives to another they want to mate, to show off their strengths and assets. To prove themselves as a good partner, like with hunting. Like the rabbit."

Rhys had a feeling he already knew, but— "What's a mate?"

Everett smiled weakly up at Rhys. "It's...someone that a wolf shifter loves, someone they want to spend the rest of their lives with."

Oh. *Oh.* "So...exactly like a marriage proposal, then." Rhys couldn't stop the relieved bit of laughter puffing out as he held Everett's gaze. "You want me to be your mate? You want to spend the rest of your life with me? Is that what the rabbit means?"

"Yes, I do," Everett whispered quietly, yet his tone was unwavering and sure. "As long as you do too."

Rhys couldn't believe it. They had both expressed their feelings toward each other, even going as far as declaring that they belonged to each other, but it hadn't quite sunk in that Everett was 100 percent serious in that declaration. A part of Rhys, deep inside, was still convinced that someday, Everett would be happy to leave him, ready to run wild and free in the forest like the other wolves. Yet here he was, asking to be with Rhys forever, wanting to be his mate.

Oh god. He was going to be a werewolf's mate. Now it really seemed as if he was in *Twilight*. Was he the Bella to Everett's Jacob?

"Wait... It's not like in *Twilight*, right? You didn't 'imprint' on me like weird ass Jacob did with Bella's baby? Because that...that would be too much."

"Pfft, no. Wolf shifters don't do that. Sure, we usually mate only once—unless our mate dies—but mates aren't this predestined thing." Everett giggled before his tone shifted back to a serious one.

"Please don't feel pressured to be my mate, Rhys. I promise you, you can say no at any time."

"Of course I want to be your mate," Rhys said with a sniffle, his tone just as watery as his eyes, which he hadn't realized had begun to leak tears. "I've never wanted anything else this much in my life. L-love you so much, Everett. I wanna be with you forever."

Everett smiled widely, gleeful and powerful enough to rival the sun. A calloused, warm hand caressed Rhys's cheek, gently holding his chin and pulling his face closer into a soft, tender kiss.

"Me, too, Rhys," he whispered against his lips. "Me too."

Before Rhys realized it, Everett had picked him up from his chair bridal-style in his arms—how fitting—and walked them back over to the bed. He laid him down, never once breaking the kiss that quickly grew much less languid and much more passionate. They hadn't kissed much since Everett's return, but their lips moved in sync so easily, a rhythm vibrating throughout their entire bodies. Soon, their tongues joined in to dance and taste every surface they could touch.

Though Everett covered Rhys's smaller body, not once did he exert any force to press him into the bed or hold him down, which Rhys was thankful for. Everett braced himself with bulging arms that Rhys couldn't help but reach up and stroke. They'd lost a lot of muscle mass thanks to the starvation, but they still felt so solid against his fingers, so dependable and strong.

"Having fun down there?" Everett chuckled when they pulled apart momentarily to catch their racing breaths. His dark-brown eyes sparkled like precious jewels, which Rhys wanted to hoard like a selfish dragon. But instead, he only burned as if touched by a dragon's flame, his cheeks bursting into red at being caught.

"Don't be embarrassed," Everett rumbled, pinching Rhys's cheeks when he noticed the blush. "You can touch your mate all you want."

Your mate. God, it sounded so primal, so animal, and Rhys fucking *loved* it.

"My...mate," Rhys tried the words out, forming the syllables slowly, savoring them, as he snaked his hands under Everett's shirt. What he found there had his mouth watering. He didn't have cut abs, but his torso was firm and smooth, with the sparse happy trail of hair that led down to the best treasure of all.

"*Rhys*," Everett moaned, throwing his head back when Rhys cupped his length through his sweatpants, and he quickly hardened in his warm grasp. Before Rhys could begin to stroke, though, his wrist was quickly caught. "Rhys, w-wait, *stop*, we can't d-do this right now."

"What— *Oh fuck*, I'm so sorry!" Rhys squeaked, wrenching back his hand as if burned, eyes widening. The word "stop" was like a brick thrown at his head, knocking him out of his lustful haze to realize that *holy shit he'd just been fondling Everett's dick without permission.*

What the actual hell was wrong with him, getting so ahead of himself? Getting so entranced in Everett's tantalizing body that he'd gone so far as to act like some kind of fucking sex-crazed maniac?

It had only been a couple of months since Everett had returned, only been two *minutes* since he'd accepted Everett's mating proposal, so it might've been a bit too much too soon to jump into the sexual side of things. Sure, Rhys had had his hookups before, where he'd been fucked by men whose names he didn't know, but hookups were hookups, nothing special. Not like this. This was special, something that didn't need to be rushed, something to savor. Why in the hell did he think even for a second that what he'd done was remotely okay?

God, Everett must've thought he was an asshole. Rhys wouldn't blame him if he decided he wanted to call off their relationship. Hell, he would've, too, if someone he loved had betrayed his trust so easily and badly. Everett had said he could touch him, but not like that!

"Rhys, calm down!" Everett exclaimed, shaking him by the shoulders—since when had he started hyperventilating? "Calm down, o-okay? Look, I'm sorry for interrupting you, but I wasn't rejecting you or anything; I promise!"

"Y-you weren't?" Rhys stammered out, still very much upset but also extremely confused as he peered up at Everett's worried frown. Why was he looking worried? Why wasn't he pushing Rhys away, screaming at him, cursing him to hell like he deserved? "But I was assaulting you—"

"That isn't what happened at all," Everett said quickly. "You *did not* assault me, Rhys, not at all. I told you that you could touch me. Stop overthinking everything and thinking such bad things about yourself, okay?"

"You didn't say I could touch your—"

"Rhys, *please* let me finish." Everett sighed, placing a comforting hand on Rhys's knee. "Don't put words in my mouth. I am not angry at you; you did not assault me—far from it, okay? I *wanted* you to touch me. I still do, very much so. Just..."

He took in a deep breath, cheeks reddening. "I...can't engage sexually with you right now. It's against tradition. We have to wait until my rut, okay?"

Rhys blinked, his head spinning with many conflicting emotions. "Your...rut? Isn't that, like, a deer thing, though? The instinctual seasonal drive to mate that makes bucks go feral and fight with one another over females?"

Everett nodded hesitantly. "Yeah, it's kinda similar to that, I guess..."

"Huh..." Rhys said, furrowing his brow. "I didn't know that was a thing wolves experienced too. I thought there were mating seasons when the females would be fertile. And aren't mating seasons much earlier, like when winter first starts? It's already spring now!"

"Well, it's not a normal wolf thing," Everett explained, "but us wolf shifters experience it when we become adults, and we do it in the middle of spring because... Well, we need it to be warmer because we...mate as humans, and the woman is a human while pregnant until the pups are old enough to shift.

"During, um, mating season, the males go into rut and the females into heat. It's...a very, *very* in-intense desire that lasts a week." Everett's entire face turned a bright red as he vehemently avoided Rhys's gaze. "So, in our packs, it's just the two parents and all of their pups. While the parents hide away to...um, be together...their of-age sons leave the pack in search of females from other packs, mate with one, and start up a new pack. Well, that's what most of them do...ha." Everett let out a small, anxious laugh. "Except for me, that is."

"What did you do instead?" Rhys asked carefully, squeezing Everett's hand to comfort him, hating how he looked so small and afraid, shrinking in on himself.

"Remember how I said I was kicked out? Well, that was because of what I 'did instead.' Last spring was my first ever rut, which I'd been really looking forward to so I could escape my shitty pack. Once it hit, I left to look for some females... But with every single one I met, I wasn't attracted to them like I should've been. I don't know why, but I just...*couldn't*."

Everett squeezed his eyes shut as if the memory pained him. "I felt so fucking *ashamed* going back to my pack, being greeted by my sisters... None of my brothers had ever come back. They teased me, saying the reason I didn't get a mate was because I was so small, weak, and ugly...that something was *wrong* with me. And maybe there was. When a shifter from a neighboring pack came by to take one of my sisters, he was the first wolf I was ever attracted to. A *male* wolf. My rut was so, *so* strong just from looking at him, and I couldn't stop myself from trying to flirt with him, to convince him to take me rather than my sisters.

"But, of course, he didn't want me. And, of course, when my parents came back and my siblings ratted me out to them, they didn't hesitate to kick me out. They didn't want to have a weak, weird, *gay* son around. And I...I don't blame them."

"Everett..." Rhys sighed, pulling him into a tight hug at the first few tears running down his face. Everett sobbed into Rhys's chest, grasping his sweater in tight fists as if his life depended on it. "Don't talk about yourself like that. Being gay is not bad, *at all*. Fuck tradition and fuck biology, okay? Do not be ashamed for liking what you like. Do you think I'm weird for being gay?"

Everett shook his head feverishly. "N-no..." he whispered between sobs.

"No, I'm not. And neither are you. Your pack was wrong to say and do those things to you. I'm so, *so* sorry you had to go through that. It's not fair, and I doubt it was fun to be rejected either." Rhys stroked one hand through Everett's hair and the other over his back.

"It felt like *shit*," Everett growled. "He looked at me with so much fucking disgust. I hated it."

"Well, fuck that dude, and fuck your entire pack! They're the weird ones!" Rage boiled inside Rhys just thinking about how awful his poor Everett had been treated for such a bullshit reason. He couldn't imagine what it would have been like if his parents had been homophobes on top of being unempathetic about his disorders.

"Honestly," Rhys continued, "I'm glad they kicked you out so you wouldn't have to withstand that any longer. Glad because you got to meet me. Because I'd never look at you like that. I only look at you with love, Everett. Love and a fucking *ton* of lust."

Everett peeked up at him. "Really? You do?"

Rhys snorted. "Was that not obvious when I was touching your dick?"

Everett's cheeks flared red once more, and he hid his face back in Rhys's sweater. "Oh my god, *Rhys*!"

"What? What's wrong, huh? I know you want me too," Rhys singsonged, a sly grin growing at Everett's endearing innocent virgin act.

"I mean, of course I do!" Everett squeaked. "Are...are you sure you're okay with waiting until my rut? And are you sure you feel strong enough to? Rhys, you only recently recovered."

"Some of the wolf traditions are outdated, like that heteronormative bullshit, but I totally understand wanting to wait. I'll always respect that," Rhys said without hesitation, leaning in to press another kiss to his lips. "And stop your worrying. I'm fine, and there's still a month or two until the middle of spring."

Rhys could've waited a few months, years, decades, however long Everett needed to feel ready. He would've even been perfectly fine if Everett never wanted to be sexual with him. Sex didn't define their relationship, after all. He didn't need sex to love Everett, to show him how much he did.

Everett pulled back again, his anxiousness and sadness bleeding into a huge, shining grin.

"Thank you, Rhys. Really. Thank you."

"There's nothing to thank me for, silly." Rhys giggled. "But, if you don't mind, since we're already talking about it, I'd love to ask you some more questions about werewolves—if you'd be comfortable answering? I want to know the wolf side of you better."

"Yeah, of course! What do you want to know?" If Everett were in wolf form, his tail would've been wagging a mile a minute.

"Well, my biggest question is, like, how has your species not been made known to humans yet?"

Everett shrugged. "I think we are really, really careful to always be in wolf form when we aren't in the den, so no humans ever see us shifted. We actually don't stay in our human forms that much. The entire winter, we usually stay as wolves since we deal with the cold much better with fur. In summer, we'd only be humans when inside the den.

"But I spent a lot more time in my human form than anyone else. While my siblings were out hunting and patrolling and stuff, I was told to stay back and do den duties, like cleaning. Like I said earlier, my pack thought I was weak and not very smart, so I didn't get to do anything cool. I wasn't even allowed to come to territory negotiations!"

"And I still think that's bullshit," Rhys said. "Weak and not smart, my ass—I wish they could see you now, shooting a bow and learning to read. You're probably smarter than all of them combined."

"Oh, stop that. I'm only good at that stuff because you're such a good teacher," Everett mumbled, his cheeks tinged pink as he waved a dismissive hand.

Rhys chuckled. "You stop that! You're smart because of *you* being such a good student. I'm not hearing any of that self-deprecating bullshit! Anyway, what do you mean by territory negotiations? How do you guys work that out? Do packs fight one another like regular wolves do?"

Everett let out a petulant whine, though he dropped the act. "Well, if regular wolves challenged us for hunting territory, the only way to settle it would be to fight, 'cuz they're not so smart. They rarely challenge us, though; they're way too terrified of us to even think about it."

He chuckled. "With other shifters, we do it civilly, talking it out in human form. Sometimes it can escalate into a fight, but usually, we work it out before it gets to that point. I wasn't allowed to attend because my parents thought I'd make our pack look foolish somehow. And of course I couldn't help in fights, being seen as weak."

Rhys cringed at the thought of his poor Everett being thrown to the wolves, literally, to be bitten, scratched, and ripped apart savagely.

"I swear, those little assholes… But I have to admit, I'm happy you never had to fight. I've seen videos of wolf fights; they look pretty nasty. That scar I gave you is enough. You shouldn't have any more marring your pretty skin." Rhys reached down to trail a finger over the scar through Everett's pants, making him shudder slightly.

His lips pulled into a wide smirk, showing off his elongated canines, fanning a small flame of arousal burning once more in Rhys's core. God, he was so fucking gone for Everett; how would Rhys manage him in rut when even the smallest things would get him going?

"You know…" Everett said. "I actually like that scar, to be honest. Grateful for it. Because if I'd never gotten caught in that trap, I might've never gotten to be with you like this." Everett's deep voice sent shivers down Rhys's spine.

"Oh my god, when did you get so damn cheesy?" Rhys giggled, shoving Everett playfully with one arm and hiding his face with the other.

"Shut up, you love it!" Everett singsonged, pulling at him to reveal his face and place a dramatic, wet kiss on his nose.

Rhys rolled his eyes and shook his head, also unable to keep the fond grin off his face. "Yeah…I really do."

Chapter Twelve

The day finally came when neither of them were expecting it, one week later.

It was still dark, barely morning, when Rhys opened his eyes—and *hot* too, almost unbearably so, most likely the cause as to why he'd awakened so early. A disgustingly moist and thin sheen of sweat covered his body, his boxers clinging wetly to his skin, making him cringe at the sensation. For a moment, he feared his dreaded flu had returned, but he felt perfectly fine otherwise. More like it was suddenly summertime already, bringing its heat that would follow him even into the night.

A quick glance over to the fireplace proved that not to have been the cause either as its flames were low and weak, in need of another serving of wood. Rhys furrowed his brows in confusion—until Everett's body moved against his, and it all made sense.

Everett was in rut.

They had fallen asleep spooning, with Everett's larger body wrapping around Rhys from behind like a clingy koala. But instead of Everett lying still and snoring, his hips bucked slightly, pushing against Rhys's ass, and he let out deep, rumbling groans.

Rhys froze and widened his eyes—sure, Everett had warned him of his impending mating cycle. But Rhys hadn't given it much thought until now, and it was already too late for him to plan how to handle the situation, this rut. His future mate's rut. Holy shit, Everett was in rut, and Rhys was absolutely *not* prepared.

When they'd talked about it, it had seemed so much further in the future. Which wasn't bad, per se. Rhys *definitely* still wanted to be Everett's mate, no matter the timing, but his stomach twisted with anxiousness anyway. He'd had no time to think it over, to ask more questions about what was actually going to happen, what he should do to take care of Everett besides the obvious. After all, Rhys was no werewolf; he didn't know instinctively how to please a mate, and that thought scared the *shit* out of him. What if he did something wrong? What if he wasn't enough for Everett? What if, what if, what if?

Though his mind reeled, Rhys forced himself to take a long series of deep breaths, trying to calm himself down. It wasn't the time for this; there was no point in worrying and regretting all of the wasted time, not when he had his poor mate to take care of. Though he slept still, Everett was obviously in distress and pain, with his scrunched-up face and the needy, pleading sounds he was making.

Rhys knew better than to worry over little things like this. He was getting caught up in his anxiety again, even though Everett had reassured him plenty of times that Rhys would always be enough no matter the circumstance. That had to apply to this...right? Didn't it? Rhys would take good care of his mate. All he needed was to calm down, take a few more deep breaths, and—

"*Everett!*" Rhys squealed, body jolting at the sharp canines digging into the bare skin where his neck met his shoulders. It was enough to send a shock of painful pleasure through his nerves, yet thankfully not enough to break skin. Rhys strained to look down to where Everett's face nuzzled against the now sore, bruising spot, his eyes wide awake and staring up at him. "E-Everett, *ow*, that hurt! Why did you bite me?"

Everett hummed against his skin, goose bumps rising under the ministrations. "Sorry," he murmured, placing a kiss under Rhys's jaw. "Couldn't help it. You smell so *good.*"

"I do *not* smell good. I smell all sweaty and gross," Rhys grumbled.

"Mmm, tastes good too," Everett replied in the same devastatingly attractive, deep, raspy voice. He licked his lips. "Sweet and salty. I like it."

Rhys made a disgusted gagging sound at the words that quickly changed to a small, startled moan when Everett licked a long stripe up from his collarbone to his ear—a surprisingly erogenous zone that had him shuddering at the sensation of sharp teeth nibbling at the sensitive cartilage.

"God, and your *sounds*— You're killing me here, Rhys," Everett growled, not holding back in the slightest from continuously humping Rhys's clothed backside. "Even better than in my dreams."

"Oh? Were you dreaming about me, hmm?" Rhys teased, letting his eyes flutter shut in pleasure, arching his back and pushing his ass back against the relentless pressure. "Is that why you were rutting against me in your sleep? You woke me up, you know. What were you dreaming about that got you so hot and bothered?"

"Fucking you," Everett said without shame or hesitation, punctuating his words with a particularly harsh thrust that had Rhys's cock hardening in his pants. "Fuck, I want you so bad, Rhys. Want to *breed* you. Will you let me in? Will you let your mate fuck you good like you deserve?"

Rhys gasped at the dirty, filthy words. He hadn't expected his sweet, innocent Everett to be such a horny flirt, even under the influence of his raging rut hormones. "God, you're suddenly so damn bold, huh? But you can't breed me. I'm not a woman, Everett—"

"That wasn't an answer to my question." Everett chuckled darkly. "Do you want me to fuck you or not? Just because you don't have a womb, doesn't mean I won't still fill you up and bloat your stomach like you're carrying my pups. Do you want that? Are you going to be a good boy for me?"

The mental image of his flat stomach distending, skin pulled taut and round to accommodate the copious seed pumped into him *should've* disgusted Rhys. But he found it had the complete opposite effect, one of pure want and *yearning*. It might've been because of the rut pheromones seeping into his pores, or maybe just a secret kink he didn't know he had, but there was no denying it. He wanted—no, *needed*—to be full of his mate in every way, shape, and form.

He pulled off his clothing in record time, leaving him naked, panting, and begging under Everett's hungry, predatory gaze.

"Good boy," Everett purred, flashing a smirk made intimidating by the addition of his elongated teeth. He caged his body over Rhys's and began exploring every quivering inch of his mate's lithe body with his large hands, starting at the top of his head, where he carded his fingers through Rhys's sweat-matted hair and thumbed at his bottom lip.

"Such a pretty pup," Everett murmured as Rhys leaned into his burning touch. "You want this so bad, don't you? Don't even need to tell me. I can see it, so desperate."

"Please" was all Rhys could whine pathetically. He'd been called many different pet names during sex, but "pup" was new—and Rhys loved it. "Please, Everett."

"Patience now," Everett cooed with a soft kiss to Rhys's plush, parted lips. "Let me take care of you."

"B-but I'm supposed to be taking care of *you*." Rhys pouted. "I'm ready, Everett. *Please* just fuck me—*ah*!"

Once again, Rhys let loose a cry of pleasure, this time as Everett's deft fingers dove down and brushed against the perky buds of Rhys's chest, his body seizing up at the touch.

"Sensitive, aren't you?" Everett chuckled.

"D-don't make fun of me! It's b-been a long time, okay?" Rhys whined, trying to jerk away from the ghosting touches. But Everett was relentless, one hand moving to hold him down with a firm yet gentle hand on his stomach, and the other gently pinching a nipple, now dark brown, between his index finger and thumb.

Rhys's last sexual encounter had been a few months before his move—a hookup in the dirty alleyway behind a bar with a man he didn't even know the name of. It had been a long time, but Rhys didn't remember being this fucking sensitive, like an untouched, unexperienced virgin, much to his immense embarrassment. Ironic, since Everett should've been the sensitive and shy one—he was the real virgin here.

"Not making fun of you," Everett said, grinning like the wolf he was. At the same time, his soft gaze held so much affection as Rhys's eyes rolled back when he kept twisting the abused nubs. "Just enjoying the show, all for me. My pretty, sensitive pup."

Though Everett said he wasn't making fun of him, he was clearly having way too much fun watching Rhys squirm and writhe beneath him, gasping and whining uncontrollably, jolting each time Everett switched between nipples. Rhys feared he might actually come from this somehow, even though neither his leaking cock nor hole had been touched. It was as if he were a teenager again, watching porn for the first time.

Just as he was moments away from reaching his peak, Everett pulled his hand away.

"N-no, why did you s-stop!" Rhys cried, reaching out to grab Everett's hand, trying to pull it back. "That's not f-fair!"

Everett only chuckled and leaned in to press his lips against Rhys's, his petulant complaints ceasing quickly as he melted into the passionate kiss. It wasn't rough and bruising as with his past partners, but gentle, careful, caring, *perfect*, just like every other touch Everett had bestowed upon him.

Their lips fit together perfectly, their tongues moving in a synchronized dance instead of a fight for dominance. Everett might have been the predator here, the one in rut, but even now, he kept them at equal ground. The quiet sounds of their kisses filled the room, the snuffed-out fireplace no longer adding the cracking of wood. Neither of them minded, though, as the heat radiating from Everett's body was just as good at warding off the cold.

"I love you," Everett whispered when they parted, lips still touching. "Love you so much, Rhys."

Rhys swore his heart swelled just as much as his dick. "I love you, too, Everett," he panted out. "Love you more than anyone, anything. I'm y-yours, Everett."

"*Mine*," Everett growled softly. His hands dragged their way down Rhys's body, mapping out the barely-there curves, leaving little kisses all over his torso, down his thighs—pointedly ignoring Rhys's straining cock—to the backs of his knees, and even to his toes, and then back up until he reached Rhys's ass. He took hold of the plump cheeks in his large palms and squeezed, fitting perfectly. "All mine. So pretty for me, so soft and squishy, *fuck*. I've been taking real good care of you, huh?"

Rhys nodded feverishly, arching his back as much as he could to lean into Everett's touch. He was still a bit too skinny for both of their preferences, his hip bones and ribs protruding ever so slightly underneath the thin layer of fat he'd begun building up. Yet he wasn't as weak as before, now ready, able, and happy to be fucked and manhandled for the next few days.

"You're pretty, even down here," Everett said as he spread Rhys's ass cheeks apart as far as they could go, revealing his most intimate parts to his mate: his flushed, wet cock and his hole, which winked and clenched when the werewolf's hot breath panted against it.

Of course, Rhys wasn't as smooth and hairless there as he'd once preferred back in the city, instead, sporting a thick thatch of dark, curly pubic hair. He felt a bit self-conscious about it, though Everett didn't seem to mind it one bit, even seemed to love it, burying his nose in and taking a long, deep, shuddering breath.

"*Fuck*, pup, you smell even better down here," Everett groaned.

"Y-you aren't grossed out by it?" Rhys asked, his face burning with embarrassment.

Everett peered up from between his legs, brows furrowed. "Why in the hell would I be grossed out? There's nothing gross about this, pup, not in the slightest. You're fucking *perfect*."

Rhys squirmed under his gaze, unable to meet his eyes. "Most men think p-pubic hair is gross and unclean. It's more accepted to be shaved or waxed."

"Doesn't that hurt, though?"

"I mean, yeah, it can," Rhys mumbled. It *did* hurt like all hell, especially on his wallet from spending hundreds a year on getting professionally waxed to suit his exes' tastes. "But that was just the way things were. No wax, no dick, simple as that— Well, okay, maybe it wouldn't keep me from getting fucked, but there was no way in hell any dude would even think about getting his mouth anywhere near close to me if I looked like this."

"That's...that's fucking awful. Hair is *natural*, not gross," Everett growled, his grip on Rhys's ass growing tighter. "You're telling me that men would deny you for just having hair? *You*?"

Rhys nodded meekly in shame. It felt weird now that Everett worded it that way. "Y-yeah. They would."

Everett let out a low snarl, the vibration zapping through Rhys's body like lightning.

"Fuck those idiots," Everett said, shaking his head. "They didn't deserve you, if they denied you just for that. How could they? How could they not worship your body every second of every damn day when you look and smell like *this*?"

"Th-that's just your rut talking," Rhys stammered, blushing all the way up to his ears. "I'm not a god, Everett. I don't deserve to be w-worshipped—"

"Oh, pup, if only you knew how hard it was to hold myself back from fucking you for so long," Everett said, punishing Rhys's self-deprecation with a quick, sharp nibble to his inner thigh, making him cry out at the painful pleasure. "Wanted this since the first day I met you. It's not just 'cuz of my rut, not at all. Now stop your worrying, pup. Just lie back, relax, and enjoy, m'kay? I'm gonna worship you like you deserve."

And with that, Everett effectively shut the conversation down, as well as Rhys's brain, turning him into mush as he wasted no time in burying his face between Rhys's ass cheeks and licking his long, rough tongue against his winking, enticing hole. There was no way Rhys could form any sort of coherent argument or response—besides moaning and shuddering—not now, when he was getting the best rim job he'd ever had in his *life*. Not even his most skillful past partners could come close in comparison.

It wasn't about Everett's technique, which was all over the place. It was about his urgency, how he seemed to genuinely enjoy it even more than Rhys, taking pride in being the one to make his mate feel this way, to be this close on such an intimate level. Everett was a sloppy eater as always, quickly making a mess of Rhys's ass and the blankets under him, soaking them with saliva. As he licked and sucked at Rhys's rim almost desperately, he made loud, obscene slurping noises that would've had Rhys cringing if he weren't so fucking turned on. He quivered like a leaf, his hips trying to buck into the overwhelming sensation, but Everett's hands were still there to gently hold him in place, forcing him to lie there and take it like the good pup he wanted so badly to be for his mate.

It took Rhys only minutes to come from Everett's dedicated ministrations. Rhys snapped his hands down to pull his mate's coiled hair with all of his might as he painted his stomach white, eyes rolling back into his skull. The orgasm seemed to go on for what felt like forever as Everett picked up the pace with his skilled tongue, extending the orgasm far past the peak and into the land of overstimulation that had Rhys's mind growing hazy. He let out breathy, stuttered gasps as he rode the never-ending wave of pleasure.

It only intensified when Everett growled against his rim, the vibrations sending shockwaves up the base of his spine. Rhys arched as far as he could, bending like a contortionist. His grip on Everett's hair must've been painful, but he hadn't uttered a single complaint. Rhys had to forcibly pull Everett off with weak, shaking arms when he could no longer take it. Everett relented, though with a saliva-slicked pout, seeming reluctant to be separated from his new favorite treat.

"Y-*you*," Rhys said through his heavy panting. "I...where in the *world* did you learn to eat ass that good, huh? Were you lying about being a complete virgin? Because *holy fuck*, Everett, I was so close to passing out right there!"

Everett's pout quickly morphed into a shit-eating smirk, and he looked extremely proud of himself. "Nope.

Never done that before in my life; I swear. I guess I just have a natural talent for it. A prodigy like I am with the bow, maybe?"

Rhys scowled at his cockiness, shoving him. "Shut up. I swear to god—"

"Oh, are you swearing to yourself?"

"*Everett!*"

Everett cackled heartily, throwing his head back and smacking at the blankets while Rhys stared him down with a displeased glare, crossing his arms over his chest, waiting for him to stop.

"You're unbelievable. Why do I love you again?"

Once Everett managed to catch his breath and settle down, he smiled knowingly. "Because I eat you out so good, of course. Oh, stop your glaring, pup. You know you love me."

"Never said I didn't," Rhys grumbled quietly in defeat. "Now, are you going to keep yapping or are you going to get back to 'worshipping' me, huh? I thought you were in *rut*, Mr. Werewolf."

"Ready for another round already?" Everett raised an imploring eyebrow. He was obviously not done teasing his poor mate, though he also seemed unable to deny a clear invitation, not with his rut hormones still surging through his body. It seemed as though the need to fuck Rhys senseless had abated slightly as a result of his orgasm, but once Everett's gaze caught how Rhys's cock had begun to chub up again, it came back full force, his wolf persona taking the reins once more with a devilish, dark grin. "I thought you'd need more time to recover, but okay, if you insist. Are you *that* desperate for me, pup? Can't even wait another minute, hmm? You'll have to be patient for a bit longer though. I gotta get you all stretched out first. Are you going to be a good pup for me?"

Rhys widened his eyes, and he nodded quickly, not hesitating to spread his legs as wide as they could go to present himself, wincing slightly at the stretch in his muscles. "Yeah, gonna be your good pup."

Everett growled, pleased, at the sight of his mate. "Pup, do you have something we can use to get you all wet for me?"

"Yeah, yeah, lube, I have lube," Rhys rushed out, wanting to get a move on already. "It's under the bed, in the little brown box."

Everett took one long, hungry look at Rhys before ducking to retrieve the box. He then opened it to reveal the treasure within. It didn't just have lube; there were toys as well: two large dildos and one vibrator. Rhys hadn't had the chance to use them for a while as he couldn't play with himself with Everett always around. They must've still smelled like him, though, evident when Everett couldn't hold back a snarl as he took in a deep breath and pulled out the large half-empty bottle of lube.

"Naughty, naughty pup," Everett chastised, tossing the box aside. "I didn't know you were that *dirty*."

"Th-there's a lot you don't know about me. And I didn't know you were either," Rhys said haughtily.

His eyelids fluttered shut at the cold touch of lubed fingers prodding at his welcoming hole, two of them slowly nudging their way in. Larger than his own, they brought a simmering burn that made Rhys grit his teeth in the best way. Everett was careful with his movements, delving all the way in and pulling out gingerly, only scissoring his fingers once the creasing between Rhys's eyebrows softened and dispersed from the discomfort fading into pleasure.

"Well, I plan to find out every little detail. Like...let's see. How many fingers can you take?"

Getting a third and then a fourth finger in was somehow much easier than the first two, the thick ring and pinky fingers sliding in snugly next to the middle and index. They reached deep inside Rhys, poking and prodding and stroking, seeming to familiarize themselves with his velvety, warm walls, mapping them out. Everett soon found Rhys's prostate, making Rhys gasp and clench hard around his fingers when the tip of his middle one jabbed against it. For a moment, Everett looked confused, likely unaware of the complexities of human male anatomy. But Rhys's face—fluttering eyelids and drool escaping from the corners of lips pulled up into a dopey smile—only showed immense pleasure. So, Everett continued to massage the spot, paying special attention to it.

"Is that good, pup?" Everett smiled fondly, speeding up the pace of his ministrations. "Do you think you can take more?"

Rhys was almost too out of it, mind too hazy with a second impending orgasm, to answer, though he yelped and nodded when Everett asked a second time, whispering the words directly against his ear, punctuating it with another nip. Rhys didn't know why he needed to be stretched this much, but he wasn't complaining at all.

The fifth finger—which was Everett's entire fucking *fist*—proved to be a challenge to fit in, taking what must have been almost ten minutes to ease in. The tip of the thumb entered first, making Rhys whine and then full-on cry when the knuckles joined the party, the widest thing he'd ever taken. It hurt so bad, almost like his poor rim would tear right in half. But Rhys never said for it to stop, no matter how many times Everett asked if he wanted to. Eventually, his walls molded to the shape of Everett's hand, sucking it in all the way to his wrist.

"Oh pup, look at you," Everett praised, peppering Rhys's tear-streaked face with a plethora of kisses. "You did it; you took them all. I'm so proud of you."

"Y-you are?" Rhys hiccupped, staring up at his looming mate through damp eyelashes and hazy vision. He'd always been such a sucker for praise, so even though he felt more pain than pleasure at the moment, it was enough for him to forget it for a moment, reveling in the soft look in Everett's gaze and caress against his jawline. He was proud of himself as well, having never fit anything this large in him before, almost the width of two of his dildos.

"Mm-hmm. And you know what else?"

"Wh-what?"

Everett's smile grew even bigger. "I think you're ready for my knot now, perfectly stretched."

Rhys hadn't been expecting Everett to have a knot like a real wolf, but it wasn't something that scared him in the slightest. In fact, it sounded downright wonderful. He gurgled in happiness at this revelation, something primal inside him pleased with the idea of being stuffed so full by his mate's cock. Sure, he was no werewolf, but that didn't matter as long as he could take everything Everett would give him and love it all the same. He was *enough*; there was nothing to worry about.

"My perfect mate," Everett said as he shifted his fist, knuckles grazing Rhys's prostate. "Does it hurt? Are you sure you're okay and want this?"

There was no denying that it still hurt, but the longer his rim stayed stretched, the less painful it felt, subsiding into more of an uncomfortable ache than a series of lightning strikes of sharp agony. With the stimulation to his prostate—and the hand that moved down to wrap around his cock—Rhys came a second time with a silent cry, moans eaten up by Everett's kiss.

"I guess that's a yes then." Everett chuckled once Rhys came down from his high. "God, how can you sound so cute and sexy at the same time?"

He eased his fist out, leaving him much too empty after being so amazingly *full*. Thankfully, Everett didn't leave him like that for very long, responding to his begging mewls.

Within seconds, Rhys was stuffed until close to bursting with cock. The knot hadn't formed yet, and Rhys wasn't as stretched as he'd been with the fist, but Everett's cock was still a significantly monstrous intrusion, longer and thicker than any human male could ever dream.

"Holy *fuck*," Rhys gasped, feeling as if he'd been punched in the stomach, all the air knocked from his body when Everett sheathed himself fully. He reached up to dig short fingernails into Everett's shoulders, to ground himself so he wouldn't come a third time just a minute after the last. "You're so *big*, Everett."

"And you're so little. Yet I fit inside you perfectly. *Mine*. My little pup, my mate, all for me."

From then on, no words were spoken—Rhys, too fucked out and overwhelmed to form a sentence let alone a single coherent word, and Everett, too lost in the effects of his hormones to do anything but growl and snarl and *fuck*. It was primal, instinctual, rough—yet at the same time, intimate and soft.

The harsh thrusts and slapping of skin contrasted with their kisses and caresses. Love bubbled up inside them, threatening to spill over. Over the last few months, it had grown stronger, harder to ignore until it was impossible to hold it back. Everett sank his sharp canines into the delicate skin of Rhys's neck, just below his ear, as his knot swelled and locked, marking Rhys as his mate inside and out.

Rhys, not expecting the bite, screamed himself hoarse when the teeth sliced cleanly through his skin to fill Everett's mouth with his scorching blood. It was so much—*too* much, combined with the knot, the never-ending waves of thick come pulsing deep in his guts, and his own come painting both of their stomachs—yet he took everything Everett gave him and held it deep within himself, forever grateful for the trust and love they shared. His stomach swelled with the evidence of the sheer volume of come inside him, rounding like a pregnant woman as Everett had promised. It should've scared him, but it *didn't*. Nothing Everett could ever do could scare him. Everything he did was out of love, and in that moment, it was all Rhys could want.

Absolutely exhausted and shrouded in the haze of multiple orgasms, Rhys let Everett move his boneless body, flipping them over so they spooned, careful not to crush his mate, tug on the knot, or put pressure on his distended stomach. As Everett stroked his big hands up and down, he planted kisses on every part of Rhys he could reach, growling softly under his breath in a way that could only mean he was content and sated.

For now, at least. Because this was only knot one and day one, with plenty more to go.

★

The next few hours went by in a similar fashion as the intensity of Everett's rut increased, clouding his sanity with pure lust. After only a few minutes for Rhys to rest, Everett was raring to go yet again.

Rhys's rim had become quite sore and his throat raw from so many loud, pleasured screams. So, after the third knot had deflated, he was relieved when it seemed as if the exhaustion had taken a toll on Everett as well. They both hissed as he gingerly pulled out of Rhys and then carefully moved to the side so he could lie down next to him. Immediately upon his head hitting the pillow, Everett's eyes closed, and he fell asleep, leaving Rhys to chuckle when the snoring began within seconds.

"I'm tired as fuck, too, but I guess *I'll* be the one to take care of us and clean up," Rhys grumbled as he stood, then almost fell due to the weakness in his muscles.

Thankfully, he was able to walk over to the kitchen despite the soreness between his legs. He grabbed two glasses full of water, a few big pieces of deer jerky, and a wet towel to bring back to the bed. He carefully swiped it all over his body, trying to remove the nasty dried sweat, lube, and cum that covered him in a sticky layer. Once he was done with himself, he moved on to cleaning Everett.

As he gently dabbed at his mate's soft cock, Rhys marveled at how big it was even now. How had that thing, and the knot, managed to fit inside him so perfectly, jabbing at his abused prostate with every thrust? God, he was already horny again just remembering how it felt, even though he was so sore, tired, and probably didn't have anything left to come. It was almost as if Rhys were the one in rut. But he wasn't. Everett was, and right now, he needed to eat and drink before his rut would inevitably flare up again.

"Hey, baby, wake up," Rhys whispered as he shook Everett's shoulders.

It took a few moments for him to awaken, his eyes fluttering open. Once he saw Rhys hovering above him, his lips pulled into a dopey smile.

"Oh, hey there, pup," he drawled. "Are you already ready for more?"

Rhys snorted, swatting Everett's hands away when they went to grab for his ass.

"Calm down, horny wolf. We can again later. You must be exhausted—hungry and thirsty too. Here, have at these. It's been hours since we last had any sustenance." Rhys handed him one of the cups and a piece of jerky, as well as grabbing some for himself.

"I should be the one getting these for you, taking care of you," Everett grumbled under his breath, though he did as he was told, devouring the jerky.

After they'd both finished, Everett wasted no time in pulling Rhys back into his embrace, lying on their sides with their chests touching.

"How are you doing, pup?" Everett asked softly, pushing back Rhys's sweat-matted fringe, his eyes shining with so much love it made Rhys blush.

"I'm okay. More than okay, actually. I came like...ten times, so of course I feel good! And how are you? You seem a lot more...human now."

"I'm really glad you did, and so did I. Really, really good." Everett grinned, but it soon fell into a small frown. "But I...I didn't hurt you...right?"

Everett pulled back to scan Rhys's naked body up and down. His frown only deepened when he took in his roughed-up state. Everett had really done a number on him with his hands and mouth, leaving speckled bruises not just on his neck and chest, but also on his legs and his ass. But what was really concerning was the deep, ugly bite wound on Rhys's neck, still crusted with blood, and it almost made Everett's eyes pop out of his head in shock.

"Shit, oh fuck, did I *bite* you?" Everett squawked as he jumped up from the bed, fell onto his knees, and descended into an apologetic bow. "I'm so, *so* fucking sorry Rhys. I swear I didn't mean to. I was trying to hold myself back. I didn't even warn you this might happen—holy shit, I bit you— Wait, wh-why are you laughing?"

Rhys covered his mouth with his hand, trying to suppress the giggles. "Sorry, sorry. I shouldn't laugh. You just...you just look so funny kneeling there all naked with your dick hanging out."

"I—what? Are...are you not upset? I bit you! I hurt you. I made you bleed!"

"Everett, baby, get up off the floor and come back here." Rhys said, motioning with a weak arm.

Hesitantly, Everett got back on the bed, but he sat with his head hung low and the farthest he could from Rhys. Sighing, Rhys mustered up the remaining strength in his body, scooted over to him, and lay his head on his lap so Everett would be forced to look at him.

"Listen to me," Rhys said, holding their eye contact steady. "It's okay. I'm fine, I've had much worse wounds than this before. I promise you; I don't mind. But can I ask...*why*? Why did you bite me?"

Everett stared intently at the bite, a perfect scar in the shape of his teeth, before sighing. "Promise you won't get mad?"

"I think if I were going to be mad, I would be by now." Rhys smiled encouragingly. "I promise I won't be."

"It's..." Everett gulped. "It's a, er, mating bite. It's what werewolves do when they, uh, want to claim and mark their mate, showing everyone they're taken. It's instinctual...b-but that doesn't make it okay. I didn't even warn you about it—"

"Hey, hey, calm down. Don't you get all worked up again," Rhys said slowly. "You're fine, I'm fine, we are okay. I'm not mad, all right? Sure, I wasn't expecting it, and it hurt like a bitch—stop those fucking sad puppy eyes, I'm not finished—*but* I'm happy you did it."

Everett blinked, dumfounded. "You...are? Happy?"

Rhys snorted and rolled his eyes. "Duh, of course I am. I'm flattered you think of me that way...like I'm your mate. For real, on your werewolf-y level. But I have to ask..." He paused, taking in a deep breath. "You won't regret this...right?"

Everett shook his head feverishly. "What? Why would you think that? Why would I ever regret mating you?"

"I dunno." Rhys shrugged. "Because I'm not a werewolf, Everett, not even a woman. Wouldn't you rather mate someone who can give you pups? Start your own pack with?"

It had been weighing on Rhys's mind for some time now. Even though handling Everett's rut and receiving his bite had soothed his worries immensely, the truth of his biology was still there. He could never, ever give him pups of his own. And according to all of his biology books, and Everett's own words, mating was done to have pups and create a pack. So why wouldn't Everett be any different? Sure, he loved Rhys *now*, but what about in a few months? A year? Ten years? He would want kids someday, or at least to live with other wolves, the desires eventually outweighing his feelings for Rhys. Then Everett would leave to run into the sunset with some tramp of a werewolf, leaving Rhys to die alone—

"Hey, stop biting your lip; you're gonna make it bleed." Everett took ahold of his mate's jaw and leaned in to press a kiss there, knocking Rhys out from his stupor. "And stop your worrying too."

"B-but—"

"Rhys, I promise you, you have nothing to worry about," Everett urged. "*Nothing*. I wouldn't have mated you if I wasn't 100 percent sure I'd want you for the rest of my life. I made my decision, and it's final. *I want you*. And nobody else, no werewolf, no human, no one. I love *you*. First of all, I have no desire to go back and live in a wolf pack. And fuck having pups, okay? Did I ever even say I wanted any? And have you forgotten that I'm gay?"

Well, fuck. Rhys couldn't recall a single time Everett had ever mentioned wanting the company of other wolves, let alone pups. "No..."

"*No.* That's right, I haven't. And I don't. I don't want kids and never have wanted any." Everett kissed Rhys again, then pulled back with a dopey grin on his face. "Besides, why would I need them when I already have my pup right here?"

Rhys couldn't hold back his gummy smile and giggles when Everett pinched his flushed cheeks, trying to squirm away and hide his face in his mate's broad, comforting chest. "Shut up, you're so embarrassing," he whined. "I'm not a pup!"

"Uh-huh, *sure* you aren't, but you're just as cute as one! Look at these adorable chubby cheeks! A pup! And don't pretend you don't like the nickname. You sure liked it when I was knot-deep."

Rhys tried to scowl and be annoyed at his mate, but his bravado didn't last long, and he broke into a fit of laughter once more.

God, he loved this annoying werewolf too much to ever be mad at him.

Chapter Thirteen

Throughout the week, neither Everett nor Rhys had a full eight hours of sleep. They'd only get a few hours in before Everett's rut would flare up again, and he'd shake Rhys from sleep to envelope him in lust. So, after the week ended and his rut had completely subsided, the couple spent almost an entire day dead asleep, a much-needed rest for them both.

While Rhys enjoyed being woken up to Everett's burning gaze and touch, he had to admit waking up to the soft morning light filtering in through the curtains was almost as nice. Well, it would've been even nicer if it weren't for how damn cold it was in the room. Now that Everett's body heat had lowered back to normal, there was nothing to keep Rhys warm since the fire in the hearth had died out much earlier in the week. The cold caused goose bumps to rise on Rhys's naked, shivering body. A glance over at Everett confirmed he was affected by the cold as well as he lay hidden underneath the pile of blankets, curled up in a ball. So, even though Rhys would've loved to fall back into sleep with him, he forced himself to get up and get the heat going so his poor mate wouldn't have to suffer any longer.

His mate. God, did that sound both trippy and perfect at the same time. As though they'd just gotten married and run off together to have a vigorous honeymoon, but thankfully, with no one to bear witness. Rhys didn't have a fancy ring on, but he now sported a healing bite on his neck that was even prettier in his opinion, one he couldn't help but stop to admire for a moment in the little mirror on top of his dresser, stroking it lovingly with a big grin on his face.

After throwing on some clothes, he quickly hoisted a few logs into the fireplace and lit the charcoal and tinder with a match, watching as they erupted into dancing flames that quickly filled the cabin with comforting warmth. Next, Rhys grabbed the kettle and took it into the kitchen to fill with water, wanting a nice cup of hot tea ready for when Everett eventually woke up as well. But, before he could pour it, a familiar blur of color from the corner of his eye stopped him right in his tracks. With wide eyes, he snapped his gaze to the kitchen window. A little blue jay, perched on the windowsill, had him immediately hyperventilating.

He staggered backward, bumping into the table, eyes locked on the bird that softly trilled an eerily familiar tune. Though he thought he'd broken free from the clutches of his nightly terrors, the appearance of the blue jay proved otherwise. An omen of desperation, despair, death—and cold. Was that why he felt so cold this morning? Because he'd been lying next to his mate's frozen body?

He ripped his gaze from the bird and, almost tripping over his own feet, scrambled back to the bed. There Everett was, just like in his nightmares, hidden under the blankets. Once Rhys inevitably wrenched them off, he would be greeted with the terrifying sight of Everett's face coated in an icy film, his mouth forever stuck in a soundless, fruitless scream for his mate to come save him. Rhys didn't want to look, he didn't, he *didn't*, but his shaking hands moved of their own accord, pulling away the blankets to reveal—

"Rhys?" Everett groaned huskily, his dark brown irises peering up at Rhys so fondly, so warmly. So *alive*.

Confused, Rhys gasped, looking back and forth between Everett and the blue jay. His mind raced, trying to process the conflicting information. The blue jay was there, yet Everett wasn't frozen and dead. Was this some sort of distorted version of his nightmare?

"Rhys, hey, calm down," Everett said, quickly grabbing Rhys by the shoulders and forcing him to sit on the bed. He could feel Everett's warmth even through the material of his sweater. "It's okay, calm down. You're not dreaming; whatever you're thinking isn't real. But I'm real, Rhys. Look at me. I'm real, I'm alive, and so are you."

"B-but..." Rhys squeezed his eyes shut. "The blue jay...it's...wh-why else would it be here?"

"Rhys." Everett sighed. "It's *just a bird*. That's it. Birds exist outside of your nightmares, you know."

"But...but..."

"Rhys. Open your eyes and look at me."

Hesitantly, Rhys cracked open one eye, then the other, to gaze upon Everett's face only inches away. His puffs of breath were warm against Rhys's skin and his face was tinged a healthy pink instead of a deathly blue. Rhys slowly lifted his hand to cup his cheek, his thumb stroking the softness as Everett leaned into the touch.

"See, Rhys? It's not a nightmare. This is real life, and I'm okay," Everett whispered. "Just calm down. I know the bird scared you, but it's okay; I promise. Take in deep breaths for me."

"I-it's okay..." Rhys croaked out between breaths, repeating the words over and over again until his heart rate finally slowed to normal, and he slumped into his mate's hold.

"There you go, that's better." Everett maneuvered them so Rhys lay on top of him. He stroked up and down his back, letting Rhys feel the comforting vibrations of his voice.

"I'm sorry..." Rhys mumbled, nuzzling against his naked skin. Everett smelled good, like the pine soap they used to wash themselves with. "I thought I was finally done with those annoying nightmares...but I guess not. I'm sorry I woke you up like that."

"Hey, there's nothing to be sorry for. It doesn't annoy me at all. I'm always gonna be here to help you through them as long as that's what you want from me."

Rhys pulled back enough to kiss Everett's nose. "And I'll always appreciate your help. You've been getting really good at soothing me and my panic attacks."

"Really? I have?" Everett's lips pulled into a wide smile.

"Mm-hmm, you have," Rhys said, matching his smile with his own. "Usually, people touching me and talking to me only makes it worse. But with you...it only makes it better. Brings me back to earth, you know?"

"I'm really glad to hear that. I try hard to be good for you."

"You're better than good. You're perfect in every way possible."

They lay there for a while longer, neither caring about the time, just basking in the comfort of each other's love—before Rhys realized something, jerking up suddenly.

"Wait, oh my god! If real blue jays are here, then that means—"

He ran over to the door and yanked it open with a gasp. "There's no more snow!"

Though spring had started weeks ago, it had still been cold enough for the winter snow and ice to stick. But now, it had become just warm enough for it to finally melt away for good, replacing endless white with green as far as the eye could see. Grass poked out of the wet, muddy earth, the resilient plants growing as though there had never been a sheet of ice in the first place. Trees bore tiny buds and leaves now home to many species, such as the blue jay that had created a nest up in the closest one. The scene was absolutely beautiful and welcome, especially when only months ago, Rhys had believed he wouldn't live to see even the first blade of grass.

A quick, loud series of thumps came from behind Rhys, and Everett charged forward, running outside bare naked, giggling excitedly all the way.

"Freedom!" he cried out, arms spread in a victory pose as he slid across a mud puddle on his knees.

"Everett!" Rhys squawked. "What the fuck are you doing, you idiot? Did you forget that you're *naked*?"

"Doesn't matter, 'cuz I'm gonna shift anyway!" Everett countered, throwing a smirk over his shoulder before his human body morphed, in a split second, into that of a familiar wolf. He then lay down on his back in the mud, rolling around to coat all of his fur, his tongue lolling out of his mouth and tail wagging furiously.

"God, what is it with you and mud? You're so silly," Rhys chuckled, shaking his head. "I'm only giving you the time it takes for me to get in some better clothes and eat, and then you better be out of there when I come back out!"

When Rhys returned outdoors, wearing a big coat and a pair of jeans he didn't care too much about, the wolf sat on the porch patiently, as instructed, albeit completely covered in mud. He yipped at the sight of Rhys, suddenly jumping up in the classic position of a canine wanting to play, his butt stuck in the air and his front legs bent in anticipation.

"Hmm...you're a dirty boy, but you've been a good boy and listened to me, so go ahead. You can go run around as long as you don't play in more mud—"

Without even waiting for Rhys to finish his sentence, Everett immediately took off running through the field and straight into the woods, barking all of the way, leaving Rhys to chuckle and shake his head once again as the noise faded away.

"Well, guess I'll have some peace and quiet for a bit, then," he said with a sigh.

Stepping out into the field, Rhys slowly spun in a circle, taking in the satisfying spring scene, teeming with life. A stark contrast to only weeks prior when it'd been a frozen, dead wasteland. A thick layer of ice no longer covered the river; in fact, it flowed loudly and rapidly from all of the snow and ice that had melted higher up. The excess water would fill up all of the lakes and ponds, which would then be filled with fish once the insects returned, eventually making their way upstream. Throughout the forest, the deer had returned, climbing back up from the valleys to birth and raise their young.

They wouldn't be the only ones with new arrivals; the rabbits birthed their litters, the birds laid their eggs, and the bears emerging from hibernation might have little cubs trailing after them. It wouldn't be long until the trees and bushes began to flower and produce fruit in beautiful bright colors, just like the wildflowers that had already popped up in the grassy fields—Rhys's favorite part of spring.

Feeling as giddy as a child, Rhys practically skipped up to a particularly large patch on a nearby hill where it was less muddy. He sat in the middle of it, stroking the soft, delicate petals lovingly. A few bees, buzzing around him, thankfully didn't mind his presence.

Humming under his breath and picking a few flowers, he remembered childhood neighbors he used to play with. Every spring, he and the girls would hang out at the nearby park, picking the prettiest flowers to weave into crowns. It had been many years since he'd made one, maybe not since elementary school. But after having faced death, he decided there was no point in denying himself things that had once made him so happy.

Due to his trembling fingers, it took him much longer than it had as a child, but by the end of the hour, he had two colorful flower crowns sitting in his lap. His neighbors would've been proud of his beautiful creations, especially since his skills were so rusty. Just as he picked one up and placed it atop his curly hair, he spotted Everett dashing back from the tree line.

"Everett!" Rhys called out, cupping his hands over his mouth. "C'mere! I have a surprise for you!"

It took about thirty seconds for the wolf to reach him, panting heavily. His eyes widened when he spotted the flower crowns, and he cocked his head to the side as if to ask what they were. Chuckling softly, Rhys held the second crown up and placed it onto Everett's head.

"It's a flower crown! And don't you look cute with it on." Rhys scratched behind Everett's fluffy ear—which soon morphed into a smooth human ear.

"What about now? Do I look even better wearing it as a human?" Everett exclaimed.

Rhys couldn't hold back his snort at his mate's appearance, completely naked and covered in mud with a flower crown sitting lopsided on his coiled hair. But Rhys had to admit, the bright colors did compliment his dark skin and hair perfectly.

"I think it looked cuter on a wolf," Rhys teased with a sly smirk.

Everett's wide grin fell into a pout. "Really? It doesn't look good on me at all?"

"Nah, I'm just kidding; don't look so sad!" Rhys pushed the crown up and placed a kiss to his lips. "I mean, like, it's cute on a wolf. But on you...you look handsome, Everett. Stunning, really. I just can't take my eyes off you! Not that I want to, of course. I'd stare at you all day if I could."

"Sh-shut up!" Everett squeaked, jerking away, jostling the flower crown off his head.

Rhys let out a *tsk*. "Oh, come on, I know you love praise. What, you don't like being called pretty? Hmm, what about beautiful? Dashing? Gorgeous? Breathtaking? Hot? Attractive—"

"I-I'm gonna go wash myself off in the river. Bye!"

And with that, Everett stumbled onto his feet and raced off, giving Rhys a good look at his bare ass.

"Yeah...I'd say attractive for sure," he snickered to himself.

Chapter Fourteen

The only thing Rhys disliked about spring was how damn much it rained. Before he left for the day's hunt, he had been quite pissed off to see how his garden beds had flooded, washing away many of the seedlings he'd planted the other day; they'd have to replant them later. Though the rain had tapered off, as he trudged through the woods, his boots squelched in the deep mud. An hour into the trek, the sound was beginning to get on his nerves.

Everett, on the other hand, seemed to think the opposite. The wolf was practically prancing. Each time he kicked his paws out, he splattered mud everywhere, caking it in his fur. But Rhys did have to admit, despite being muddy as well, he enjoyed watching Everett have so much fun. They were following the scent trail of a small herd of deer that Everett had picked up that morning, and he led the way like a bloodhound. He estimated about four deer, which hopefully promised them multiple chances at securing a kill.

Eventually, Everett slid to a halt, pointing with his snout toward a clearing just up ahead, blanketed with brightly colored wildflowers and green grasses, which the deer were ravenously munching on. It had been just as rough a winter for them, leaving them too focused on filling their bellies to notice the men carefully approaching.

Rhys set himself up behind a large berry bush and pulled out his compound bow as he scanned his potential targets. At first glance, he feared that all four were does—prey he'd sworn he would never take a shot at. During this time of year, most does would've given birth, hiding their fawns in the foliage as they ate. If Rhys were to kill a doe, he'd be killing a mother—basically becoming the evil hunter who'd killed Bambi's mother in the movie. Thankfully, though, the largest of the group had tiny, almost imperceptible horns growing from its skull, signaling that it was a buck, something Rhys had no qualms in killing. It must have had one hell of a rack of antlers before its rut, ones Rhys hoped he might one day come across while hiking.

For now, the main priority was making a clean shot at the buck, which was proving to be difficult since it stood the farthest away, and the does blocked the arrow's aimed path. Rhys stood back up, forced to venture closer with Everett following. They circled the clearing, careful not to step on a twig or ruffle any branches, signaling their presence. It wouldn't be a disaster if he lost this kill, but Rhys really didn't want the eight-mile trek to end up as wasted time.

After what felt like an eternity, the men made it to the other side of the clearing without issue and set up once more behind another bush. The buck, only a few yards away now, gave Rhys the perfect shot. Quickly, he lifted his compound bow, nocked an arrow, and pulled the string back taut. But unlike the previous fall, his hands weren't steady. They quivered like a leaf in the wind, his muscles barely able to keep the string in the right position, thanks to his nerve damage. He cursed under his breath.

Everett let out a quiet whine, his wet nose nudging Rhys's hand.

"I'm fine," Rhys whispered, elbowing him away. "Just be quiet and be ready to chase it down and kill it, got it?"

Everett whined again but nodded in agreement. They turned their attention back to the buck, whose head jerked up and turned, dark eyes looking straight in their direction. It didn't flee, just stared ominously as if caught in a truck's headlights, and Rhys knew he wouldn't get a better chance than this one. He took in a series of deep breaths, attempting to will his brain not to fuck this up. He could do this. He'd killed many of deer, after all. He was a hunter.

Yet his brain didn't want to cooperate. Just as Rhys was about to let his arrow take flight, it felt as though he'd been struck by lightning, down his entire spinal column, the electric current zapping through his limbs all the way to his fingertips, which let go of the bow with a jerk. Instead of the arrow whirring through the air to lodge its sharp metal head into the buck's heart or lungs, it impaled straight through the left hind leg.

The buck and does immediately took off running into the forest with terrified calls, sounding almost identical to Rhys's own pained grunts as he collapsed into the mud. As if shocked into a state of paralysis, he couldn't move or call out to Everett, who had swiftly taken off to chase after the buck as planned. Rhys could only watch as the wolf disappeared into the thick tree line, leaving him alone, in pain and hyperventilating.

God, he was so damn frustrated with himself. As Rhys tried to gain control of his body, he was able to curl up in a fetal position. He had already been annoyed by his hands constantly shaking, but his nerve damage hadn't been that much of a hindrance to his daily life until now, acting up at precisely the worst moment possible. Sure, he and Everett wouldn't necessarily starve without this kill, since there were plenty of other things they could hunt, but this was the first time since he'd learned to use a bow that he had completely fucked up his shot. His *perfect* shot, one that would have killed the buck quickly.

While a leg shot wasn't usually fatal, it would certainly cause the buck extreme pain, leaving it lame and suffering in agony. Still, even with its slower pace, there would be no way Everett, a single wolf, could kill it. Only a pack could take down a buck as large and strong as that one. If Everett caught up with it, the buck would surely fight back, striking out with its powerful legs, which could kill him easily. Holy shit, Everett might *die*, and it would be all Rhys's fault—

A familiar whine and a wet nose bumped against his hand, knocking him out of his reverie. Rhys opened his eyes to see Everett hovering over him, blood dripping from his snout onto Rhys's sweater, and the buck's corpse sprawled out a few feet away, its throat ripped open. Rhys flickered his gaze between it and the wolf, eyebrows furrowing.

"You...you actually k-killed it? A-all by yourself? How—"

Everett cut him off with a roll of his eyes and a huff, as if to reprimand him for even thinking for a second the wolf was incapable of finishing this hunt. He then used his snout to gently unwind Rhys's curled body, pushing him onto his back, and plopped down on top of him.

"E-Everett," Rhys rasped. "What are you doing?"

Everett leaned forward to lick a long stripe across Rhys's face, replacing the tears—ones he hadn't realized he'd cried—with reddened saliva. Rhys attempted to push him off, sputtering, but was unable to with his weak arms. So, he was forced to lie there, staring up through the treetop's canopy, with this overly heavy wolf on top of him. To be honest, the pressure was actually helping alleviate his pain, allowing him to close his eyes once more and take in proper deep breaths. He buried his hands in his mate's soft fur, methodically petting him to the beat of his slowing heart rate.

He felt...safe. He felt like everything was going to be okay.

And everything *was* okay, despite all of his worrying. Even though Rhys had fucked up his shot, he hadn't lost his kill—because Everett was there. Even though Rhys was bordering on a panic attack, he didn't completely spiral into one—because Everett was there. No longer was Rhys a lone hunter living in the woods, only relying on himself to survive, only having himself to blame when things went awry. No longer was Everett a lone wolf wandering through the woods, banished, with nowhere to go. They both had their faults, yes, but their strengths, together, made up for them. After surviving the harrowing winter, there was no situation they couldn't beat. As long as they were together.

A werewolf and a human, together. God, if someone had told Rhys a year ago that he'd eventually fall in love with a werewolf, he would have rolled his eyes and thought them out of their minds. Who wouldn't? After all, werewolves were supposed to be fantasy. And Rhys was supposed to be destined to live alone in the forest for the rest of his life, never to be loved or truly belong.

Maybe Everett was why Rhys felt so at home in the forest in the first place. Maybe that was why he felt it calling to him—Everett calling to him, begging him to come home, to find him.

Acknowledgements

I, C.D. Habecker, owe the most gratitude to my amazing cowriter, Luna Nyx. We just had our two-year friend anniversary, a friendship that started because she loved my fanfics. I couldn't have written this without her. Together, we make an amazing writing team. When I'm hit with writer's block, she's always there to reassure me and help me work through the difficult scene. She is incredibly creative and comes up with amazing story and scene ideas. She inspires and makes me laugh every day. Thank you for being my best friend. I can't wait to write more novels with you and be friends for many more years to come. I'm so proud of us! Our baby is a published novel now! They grow up so fast.

Thank you to my roommate/friend for always being there to listen to my rambles about this novel, even though you hadn't had a chance to read it yet. You always listened when I told you about random wolf facts as well, not once judging me. I'm so proud of you for graduating and following your dreams. You inspire me with your resilience and strength, and never fail to make me laugh even when my depression hits the hardest. You and Luna were my rocks and my first ever non-toxic friends, supporting me through my difficult breakup and beyond.

Thank you to my parents for always being so supportive in my writing career as well as my sexuality. You guys gave me the freedom to be who I wanted to be, whether that meant letting middle-school me put on so much eyeliner that I looked like a raccoon, or reading my pieces that I was comfortable sharing with you.

Thank you to the fanfiction community for all of the love throughout the years and for all the amazing fanfics I got to read that helped to fuel my passion. Fanfiction is often looked down upon, but there are so many incredible fanfics that I hope one day can get published as well. Every time I read comments left on my stories, I can't help but cry. You guys are so sweet.

Thank you to my second-grade teacher for rewarding me with candy and food when I'd write little horse stories. I still attribute my original kickstart into writing to you.

I'm also very thankful to the NineStar team, specifically my editor Elizabetta McKay, for seeing the potential in this novel and helping me make it even better. Even though this is my debut novel and I had no idea what I was doing in the publishing world, you were so patient and kind with me.

And, of course, thank you to our readers. I can't wait to share more stories with you all!

About C.D. Habecker

C.D. Habecker is a bisexual woman residing in Portland, where she is pursuing a BFA in fiction writing at Portland State University. Ever since she was a child, C.D. has been an avid writer and reader. Writing fanfiction helped her realize her passion for creating queer romances and spinning familiar tropes. Her favorite trope is any type of animal shifter or hybrid, with magic coming in a close second. C.D. strives to give good representation to the queer as well as disabled communities, often featuring characters who share her mental and physical illnesses. She believes that not every queer story needs to focus on the struggles and hardships of being queer, as there is more to a queer person's life than that. Everyone deserves a sweet yet deeply nuanced romance they can relate to, as well as swoon, cry, and laugh with.

C.D. spends her days writing, reading, playing with her dogs, listening to BTS, and thrifting for her vintage clothing business. You can find her on Twitter @cdhabecker and on Depop @gmovintage.

Email
cdhabeckerauthor@gmail.com

Facebook
Author C D Habecker

Website
www.cdhabecker.carrd.co

About Luna Nyx

Luna Nyx is an asexual lesbian young adult living in the Denver area of Colorado. She's currently studying to become a Vet Tech, and writes on the side as means to pursue her creative passion. She fell out of love with writing and reading as an adolescent because growing up with ADHD made school a big challenge for her, and she'd begun to associate her passions with failure and disappointment. However, after meeting C.D. Habecker, Luna rediscovered her passion for literature. Inspired by her struggles growing up and the lack of decent LGBTQIA+ representation in media, Luna writes stories to show people with neurodivergence and "queer" identities that they aren't alone.

Luna currently lives at home with her parents and spends her days studying in college, lovingly annoying her three pet cats, and burying herself in her musical and artistic passions. Her email is rabbitdelamoon@gmail.com, and her Twitter account is @lunanyxwriting. Her current website is lunanyxwriting.carrd.co.

Also from NineStar Press

Waiting for Raine by Layla Dorine

Every Gathering, Raine hides from potential mates, knowing that in a society where tri-bonds were the expectation, a wolf wanting a mate all to themselves was an anomaly.

Enter Gabriel. They'd met two years before, both left disappointed when no bondmark appeared on their wrists at that time. Gabriel's been hunting, but there's been no sign of Raine, outside of the one brief visit that didn't end the way he'd hoped for.

Fast forward to the present Gathering. He's stumbled onto Aiden, a wolf miserable in his own pack due to the way he's treated. Born with a disability, he knows he can't keep up, but no one has taken the time to teach him where his true potential lies—until Gabriel that is. Gabriel's protective instincts kick in almost immediately.

Now Gabriel has one wolf he desperately wants to care for and another who has been hiding from him. Unfortunately, it might not be a challenge Gabriel is up for.

Escape by Sean Ian O'Meidhir & Connal Braginsky

Rare male weresnake Robbie has had his whole life decided for him down to his meals. But when the time comes for him to perform an unspeakable duty to his clan, he runs.

San Francisco Pride is in full swing when technomage Theo spots a scared-looking young man with brilliant emerald eyes. He's only looking for a hookup, but before he knows why, he's taking Robbie home and introducing him to champagne and enchiladas. He doesn't have any intention of falling in love.

Robbie doesn't want to return to his clan, at least not without trying to fit a lifetime of experiences into a week, but every day he stays puts Theo in more danger. One week of freedom leads to sexual awakening and adventure... but they're going to need all their wits and Theo's magic to fight for their future.

Connect with NineStar Press

www.ninestarpress.com

www.facebook.com/ninestarpress

www.facebook.com/groups/NineStarNiche

www.twitter.com/ninestarpress

www.instagram.com/ninestarpress

www.ingramcontent.com/pod-product-compliance
Lightning Source LLC
LaVergne TN
LVHW091543060526
838200LV00036B/692